Respect My Gangsta

3

Empty the clip

By

Ms. Pantha Jones

TakeOver Publishing LLC

Gary, Indiana

Copyright©2017

Paperback ISBN#13 978-0-9824338-3-6

Copyright ©2015 Take Over Publishing LLC

Cha Copyright ©2015-2017 Ms. Pantha Jones

Cover Design- LRB

Editing- Latoya Mabon

Acknowledgements

Thank you God for everything. My family and I have truly been blessed.

RIP Angela F. Arnold, Grandpa Bland and Grandpa Jones, Terry Lee, Jeff Tyson

I thank my husband Antur Little Sr. aka My Butter for giving me the opportunity as my helpmate, spirit mate to write and create full time. Pheww, Peanut butter Black Man I love and adore me some you. I have watched you work yourself through pain to provide for us. You are appreciated and loved. A Black Man runs my household and I'm proud of it.

My Children , Diamond, Cashmere, Tyrin, Antur Jr., Anturnett, Joshua , Angeleah, Kingston, I love you.

Grandparents William and Jessie Mae Bland, Step-father Byron and Octavia Arnold

Grandparents Judge and Bessie Mae Jones, Grandparents Lenora and Daddycott Arnold

Mother and Father -In law, Valerie and Alonzo Davis

My extra babies Ty Baby , Chocolate drop, Trin and Rya and their beautiful mom Janaea, Dantriece aka My Super model . E and Destiny. RIP Kash

Shout out to my partner and her beautiful children, Mahogany Bang, TOP let's Go!, Novelist Travis VP Hunter and family, Aja Boyd and family.

3

Thank you for your support family and friends

Too many Aunts, Uncles, Cousins and Extended family members to name individual.

My Siblings-Loomis, (nephews and nieces)Jayden, Byron, Bryan, Dalton, Khloe, Kylie, D(Alicia Murray -love you tell my Jayden Hi!) and Romancia

The Bland, Jones, Arnold, Hightower, Hudson, Fisher, Davis , Mitchell, Little, Brown, Wilderness, Rimmer, Powell, Ammons, Wofford, Banks. Rodriguez,

Friends,Supporters ,Readers-Tifiane , Elaine, Roc Vega, Candi Girl, Valisia Greenwood, Charae' Burks-Bland, Ms. Christina Williams, Donna Red Williams, Tureko Straughter, Teisha Sims, Daryll Smith,Tashemia Pringle, , Darlene, Auntie Brenda, Tayjia Keener, Kieshawn Whaley, DC, Ra-Ra, Sherron Blacks(Pig), Shep,Tanisha Reed, Alex Amos(lol), Author Lalita Arnold, Black Poe, Aleta Williams, Sequaia Reed, Gabrielle Dotson, Keys No Lock Book Club , SIRR Book Club, Tiara Bland, Shep, Shanda, April, Lillie, Kesha Powell, Arkeya Keys, Keisha Passmore, Bionca Tate, Otis , Farrah HIll, J.Blanco, Keanda, Roy Glenn, Thomas Long, Avoery, Julian, Nikki Wilkins, D-Mo, Brandon Bowen, Vanessa Mitchell, Gladys Miranda and John Ramos, Emilee and the G.O.A.T. s, Martina and Mr. Carter, Ms. Marie, Sabriah, Brick House aka Carolyn, Gina "G" Perry, Deanna, Hazel Merritt,Javona Smith,Monique Burton, Allene Wofford , Kitty Johnson,Tierra Marsha KT,Mercedes Taylor, Quanisha Lenoir, Toinea Mayo,Andrea Blackstone, June Miller, Denise Ramona Boyd, Tyresha Tyler, Jasmine Barber.Demettrea, Bigmofrombflo Boyd, Samyra, Dymeka, Jasmyne MsSusanpark White,Terica

"Tyrant will always find a pretext for his tyranny."A.f.

Chapter 1

"Push, Queen! Push!" said a proud chocolate man encouraging his wife to bring forth life, the life of his first child. Looking down at his wife, she had the look of urgency, anxiousness, and discomfort drawn on her face as she pushed his seed into the world.

The young husband held fear in his heart, yet he was ready to kill and die to protect the very thing that he feared. "Crowning." That one word jolted him out of whatever fear he might have been dwelling on, and pushed it so deep that it withered away and died inside of him. He was ready; Malakai already had a blueprint for his child.

She never thought she would be a mother. Being able to take care of a little human being was lost from her. However, being pregnant before, and having nothing to show for it, but longing, she proved motherhood came naturally to her. That is why, this go round, she was all too ready for this day, the day she would feel the beautiful pain of bringing a child into this world.

They smiled looking upon the face of their baby boy, with the curls and eyes of his mother, reddish, brown, dark skin of his father, and his handsome face. This man child, in his parents' eyes was their most prized possession and their strongest weapon against the streets, or he could be their weakness, the interlude to their demise. It didn't matter what sacrifices they had to make regarding their son. They will kill and die for Hunter King Gibson.

Let the love begin

24 months later

A green, volatile substance engulfed the room, making the occupants inhale it in their sleep. The room was silent, except for the soft sounds of slumbering, until the sound of a crying child was screaming through the baby monitor, sobbing through the determined calls out to his mommy and daddy. The men with cloaked faces and dark clothes frightened the young child. Being snatched out the bed in the middle of the night terrified him. His young mind could not fathom what was going on, or why this was happening.

All he needed was his mom and

dad. If they would just hear his plea upon their comatose state, he would be saved from these boogeymen. His mind was wondering, panicking for his parents. He did not understand why they were not stopping them from taking him out the house and putting him in the back of a black van. Why weren't they running out of the house like Superheroes? "Mommy, why? Mommy, why?"

Sorrow jumped out of her slumber with her heart beating rapidly in her throat. The outside was still cloaked in black sleep as she jumped out of bed and went to the closet for her gun. She ran out of the room, knocking over the glass vase on the console table. The crash of the vase startled a sleep Malakai. His first instinct was to grab the chrome 9 he had placed in the drawer before going to bed last night.

Sorrow raced to her son's room with the gun in hand, and barged in, only to find her son standing up in his crib. His smile eased her heart. It was like he knew she was worried and reached his hands out for her.

Malakai reached the room puzzled. He wanted to know what was going on, but decided not to disturb the mother and son moment. Sorrow held her son close, whispering death threats to anyone who dared to even think of harming her son. Relief overcame her body, but in her head, she knew that something was coming, and was about to start a war. Only her most worthy adversary would cross the line of this magnitude. She had none that was alive to even attempt what she just dreamed.

Malakai was intrigued by Sorrow's instant motherly instincts. He enjoyed watching her with their son. The joy on his son's face when they interacted resembled amazement and wonder. At this moment, she was reading him to sleep.

She pointed to each word and even explained to him what the picture had in it, which was a beautiful sight in his eyes. Malakai

"Are you going to stalk us or join us?" Sorrow laughed, as she watched her husband gaze upon their special moment.

"Daddy," Hunter waved the come here motions with his little chocolate, chubby hands. Malakai's spirit always beamed when he heard his son call him that name.

"Hey, man," Malakai replied as he walked towards them with his arms and hands stretched out to receive his son. Hunter jumped into his father's arms.

Malakai fell on the bed with him in his arms, laughing.

"Are you ready for nite-nite, Lil Hunt?" Malakai laughed as he rolled over on his back, throwing him in the air.

"Nite-nite," was barely audible through the giggles and baby talk.

Sorrow watched on with the same admiration that Malakai had earlier; although that didn't last long because she was exhausted from her and Hunter's activities. She kissed both her men and headed straight for the shower, leaving them to their father and son bonding time.

Meanwhile

Outside, lurking in the shadows, sat a tinted black Crown Vic, observing and surveying their habits. He was slithering with envy as he witnessed what the young black couple were living in. It was a two-story home with 2 decks, 4 bedrooms, 5 full bathrooms, and also with his dream basement.

After following her friend, Truth, from Gary to the Gibson home, he googled the property and found out about the inside from a real estate website. The website said it was sold, but still had the details of the home listed. He had been haunting anyone that was associated with the couple, rather it was friend or foe. He was feverish with a vindictiveness that had festered and ate away at his soul, for this group, for years.

Especially for Sorrow Sanae' Hunter Gibson. That little, black girl was the beginning to his loss of respect he had at the Precinct, and out there on the streets, so in a sense, he was being haunted too by the very happiness Sorrow had in her life.

Sorrow definitely did not look like what she had been through. He wanted revenge, and he didn't care who he had to kill to do it. He was just about to leave when he noticed his next stake out pull up, and Malakai running outside towards the car.

Malakai stopped in his tracks. A disconcerting feeling suited his body, like chilling armor and made him look around. He could feel somebody watching him and discreetly pulled out his 45, cocked it as he pulled it down lower in front of him, and then looked in all directions. First, he looked quickly, then he paused and studied each area looking for some type of movement.

There wasn't a visual of anyone on their property or the neighbors across the street. Not quite satisfied with his observations, he reluctantly got in the car, and he texted his wife and told her to be cautious.

Ironically, Sorrow had headphones on listening to Scarface's, "The Diary," when the text came through. Jolting upward, the cord to the headphones snapped out of its device and the house filled its walls with bass, while the lyrics, "Rat a tat tat, then your ass hits the mother fucking floor. Here comes the white sheet," assaulted the atmosphere of the house. Sorrow instinctively reached for the

9mm holstered at the head of her bed, locked her door, and turned on the TV to the ten surveillance cameras. There was nothing indicating an intruder. Even though they would have been alerted if anyone was near the house, she still felt a sense of relief once she surveyed the monitors.

Yet, still something was telling her to physically check the house. Luckily, after the time he spent with his father, Hunter fell asleep in their room watching cartoons. She knew he was safe. She kissed him before locking the door behind her, carrying her tablet, which allowed her mobile visual, giving her the ability to see any room before entering.

Holding the tablet and the 9mm seem to be distracting, so she flicked a button turning off Scarface rapping about, "wondering why he never seen a man cry until he seen that man die," and sat it on the table at the end of the stairs. Silence hushed the whole house as she maneuvered in and out of every room with her gun drawn. She was aiming and ready to blow away anything that moved or made a sound as soon as she crossed the threshold of each room. The kitchen was the last room to check. It led to the lower deck overlooking

Lake Michigan. The house was secured. She stayed to study the darkness.

The lake and night sky seemed harmonious, engulfing their home in a peaceful surrounding. That was what Sorrow loved about moving to the serenity of Oak Brook, IL. She now had peace of mind, no gunshots in the distance, no drugs, no bullshit, and no one who knew her as Black Pantha. This was her ideal getaway, but at this very moment, she felt that something was about to happen. She underwent an eerie emotion looking into the black nothingness. Just as she was turning away, a crow landed directly in the security light, lighting up the floor of the deck. She felt the crow was a sign taunting her with her past. The sign of death was now invading her present.

Chapter 2

A soft melody echoed throughout the bedroom. Low, slow music seduced two bodies to its beat. The in and out motions of a butterscotch fit man, entering his wife made for a beautiful musical. He grabbed the back of his wife's neck, as he played with her pussy with his dick from the inside. The intensity was pleasurable. He went for her bottom lip, sucking it in, nibbling it, and in the rapture of passion, he even bit her lip and held onto it with his teeth, as he used that to fuel his heated strokes. Her moans and groans seduced his ears.

"Ma, Ma," shot its way through and killed the lovers' mood as the little, angelic voice bellowed through the baby monitor. Both laughing and panting from exhaustion, the woman tore herself away from the warmth and the hypnotic trance she was just in, to reluctantly tend to her motherly duties. She grabbed a robe and smiled at him. He licked his lips with a joyous smile on his face, as he watched his love walk out of their bedroom door.

Truth smiled as she peeked around her daughter's bedroom door to see what she was doing. Her daughter had a sad look upon her face. "Hey, Baby Girl," Truth sung, coming fully into view, and it lit up with a smile of joy as she saw her. That joy in her child's face made her forget all about the feelings she was experiencing in the other bedroom, but secretly, that moment had faded also; a hint of postpartum depression was still lingering from when Se'maj was a baby.

Now, she just knew to hide what she was feeling from her friends and family. Nobody understood what she was going through; neither did she understand the feelings that came over her. She loved her baby girl, but a sense of devastation invaded her mind from time to time.

A sense of uncertainty about motherhood.

A sense of lost identity of herself by being a mother and a wife.

She never wanted to be a mother.

She never saw herself as a mother.

Truth was selfish. She was an only child with the mother that was barely home due to work or partying. Materialistically, she had everything and then some compared to her friends with multiple children in the household. In her house, everything belonged to her until her mother got married and had step-children. That's when she decided she did not want any kids. That was when she decided she was too selfish to share.

It was times when Truth couldn't bear to hold her and left her crying in her crib for a short time. Coming to her senses, she would run and apologize to her daughter with 'I love you' I'm sorry, and a plethora of kisses. Looking at her baby girl right now made her wonder what was wrong with her state of mind, that at some fucked up moment, she could deny her sweet baby girl anything, especially a mother's love. Without her getting treatment, how healed could she actually be of this bullshit?

Nigel played sleep as he heard his wife and daughter come into the room. He smiled on the inside because he knew right now his daughter was taking steps towards him, just, so she could come and pull on his nose, beard, mustache, hair; basically, anything her little chubby fingers could get a hold of that was at her disposal. Se'maj Isis King was daddy's little girl. She could not do any wrong in his eyes. He doubts she ever would. He would blow up the world if anything ever happened to her, Nigel Jr. or Truth... any of his family.

Nigel knew something was going on with his wife when she first had the baby because she was standoffish with Se'maj. He asked around and nurses said she was showing signs of Postpartum depression. Instantly his mind wandered back to the way his mother treated Sorrow. He didn't think that Truth was anything like Chenille. Chenille was evil; however, he wanted to prevent it from getting worse. Now that Se'maj was a toddler, Truth's motherly side was showing more.

Often times, Nigel would sit in complete silence, listening to his home. The sounds were peace to him; a peace he never had in his life. For as long as he could remember, even in his childhood, it was a chaotic whirlwind, but it was something deep within him that was still disturbed by the lie he told his sister.

His intentions were good. He wanted her to have some type of peace with her past. Shit, he wanted to have peace with it as well. So, that lie changed Sorrow, for her to think that the great, Mrs. Chenille King, apologized for all her wrongdoing and torture by killing herself, and that

31

heartfelt confession she left behind healed part of Sorrow's soul in a way. To have Chenille admit to what she did, and to let her know she did not deserve to be treated like that, was in a way, to her, that Chenille was giving her the respect she always wanted. If his baby sister was happy, then he was happy, but the play out of his death came to mind. He knew his sister felt betrayed by not knowing he was still alive.

All the men in her life left her in this frigid ass world by herself to survive by herself. That was something he could never forgive himself for. He never knew the whole deal of what happened when everything went down. Everything she went through was bits and pieces to him, and he found himself going to Truth for answers.

Even though Truth herself was involved in some things, she still only had parts of the puzzle to share with Nigel. Truth and Nigel found themselves captivated by each other. Nigel only wanted to know about Sorrow, but with each story he found himself watching her full lips, fantasizing about kissing them. He found that they both held eye contact a little too long and then quickly averting them when they finally grew out of the trance. Truth and Nigel never thought of each other in that way. However, look at them now, married with a little girl seven years later.

Mrs. Truth Blazio-King, in Nigel's eyes, earned that title when she held him down throughout his bid, as his friend. He confessed to her about all the female correctional officers and Prison Nurses he was messing with at the time, and why he did what he was doing. Truth became someone he could trust when he started giving her money to give to Teesha for Nigel Jr., and without even holding her hand out. She

did that faithfully. Not once did she
pass judgment on any of his decisions,
but she damn sure was not going to hold
her tongue when she felt he was about
to mess up.

Chapter 3

Genesis pulled herself away from Sorrow's desk. Everything was in order. They were making a profit. Not quite like dirty money, but nevertheless, they were still making a healthy amount of money. They were in the works of opening a club in Merrillville, using the old club Rain. She couldn't wait for Sorrow to see the decorum of this place.

Genesis's cellphone rang for the fifth time. Sabrina was stalking her phone, as usual, around this time of day, trying to use every tactic she could to lure her home early. They were growing in distance. Let Sabrina tell it, it is because of Genesis's work ethic. Secretly, Sabrina loathed this loyalty she had for Sorrow. Loyalty that she knew surpassed the little loyalty Genesis still had for her.

Genesis attitude towards working for a friend was different from what Sabrina messy ass wanted it to be. Genesis treated Get'em Girl Creations like she herself was the CEO and founder of the clothing store. She wouldn't fuck over her business in any way shape or form, so why would she do it to Sorrow and Truth, who both are like sisters to her? Besides, she was the third owner, a little secret she kept from Sabrina's greedy ass.

Correction, they were her sisters, period. Sabrina wanted her to bring her free clothes all the time, and to bring her friends in to get free shit, or damn near free discounts. That was not going to fly, not under Genesis's watch. She did not care if the bitch's head was right every night. Business was business, and if Sabrina did not understand that, then to hell with her.

Sabrina had been suspect ever since she came up crying on her doorstep nine months pregnant. It was a point and time that Sabrina went AWOL on Genesis with no explanation. Sabrina was the first girl Genesis had loved, ever lived with, and ever took care of in her life. What hurt the most was she was pregnant by a nigga that kept beating her ass. That Genesis had pistol whipped all because of her.

Genesis remembered when Sabrina came to her doorstep after almost a year of her being missing. She just disappeared out of the blue. Genesis realized she was working too much at the shop and trying to finish up her bachelor's in accounting, so when she noticed Sabrina's presence in their home and relationship become less and less, she welcomed it because it was less arguing, and she could focus on being successful.

Sabrina was more of a distraction than a helpmate. Genesis never understood how as money-hungry as she was, she didn't know that it was hard work, dedication, and sacrifice involved in being successful and obtaining that money. It's stressful when you decide to go legit with someone that doesn't understand that legal money is not as fast to obtain like illegal money.

The team put spending, going on trips, and going out to extravagant places, on hold until all the street money that they accumulated was washed and invested into legitimate businesses. The team decided to humble themselves and live modestly, until they reign in the business world like they did in the streets.

Genesis didn't understand why Sabrina didn't understand the plan or respect it. Sabrina felt like the plan was all to benefit Sorrow. Genesis tried to explain to her that she was the one that came up with the plan.

Truth, from home, was to design signature outfits and oversee the quality of the designs. She also picked other designs to carry in the store. Sorrow, from home, handled all the interactions with buyers and sellers of the retail business. She took care of the permits, licenses, ordering and upkeep of the store. All three were fully committed to the success of their brand.

Even though Sorrow was excluded from the case, and Nigel and Malakai were home, Genesis still felt as if someone at the Gary Police Department had it out for them. Genesis wanted to make sure every aspect of their money-making was on the up-and-up and her being the accountant, she guaranteed all the i's were dotted and their t's were crossed. Getting Sorrow, Truth, and herself to fully get out of the streets was easy; however, Malakai and Nigel were a whole different story.

It's been two years since Sabrina came knocking back at her door, 9 months pregnant, and she still didn't understand the greater good of the plan or having a team. Genesis let Sabrina back in because she still had love for her, and she always wanted a child of her own. It wasn't like Genesis wasn't

44

pissed off at Sabrina's actions. She knew what type of female Sabrina was.

Often times, Sabrina tried not to be that ghetto ass hood rat because Genesis was always good to her. She treated her with respect, despite her past, reckless mouth, and her constant back-and-forth between Genesis and men. She knew that Sabrina wasn't raised like her. Her mother was for herself and nobody else, and she had no problem with teaching her daughter the same tactics. Genesis had a soft spot for Sabrina, and because of her childhood, she wanted to protect her by any means necessary.

Genesis set back in her chair, closed her eyes, and thought about the way Sabrina came back to her.

She had just came out the tub, admiring her new surroundings of tranquility and a bit of luxury she had in her new town home. She still had her Small Farms Apartment in Gary, but this was the place she went to on the weekends. Only few people knew about her home. This was her vacation home, you might say. Of course the team knew about her new home, but Sabrina didn't. Had she waited a couple more months, she would have also been able to enjoy the luxury of this town home.

The townhome was a graduation present to herself, but the furnishings and the extra luxury amenities inside of this home were gifts from her team. They knew she came here on the weekends. No one ever popped up without calling first, so she was surprised when the doorbell rung. She sat down her glass of Henny on ice, reached under her bar, and grabbed her gun, before placing it in her bathrobe pocket.

Genesis approached the door from the side, looking at the monitor screen. She paused, not believing what she was seeing. She had her hand still on her gun, as she surveyed the outside of her home to make sure there were not any surprise guests waiting for her when she opened the door.

Genesis opened the door to find Sabrina, very much pregnant, torn clothes, and bruises on her face. The tears in her eyes were genuine, but Genesis had no idea how she knew where she was and why she was there. Genesis stepped aside and let Sabrina in, mainly because this was not the neighborhood to bring out her street side. Besides, Sabrina looked like shit, and she did not want to cause attention to herself.

After that, Genesis was there for Cameron's birth. Sabrina has been there for the past year. She took care of Sabrina and Cameron; however, in the back of her mind, she didn't trust Sabrina. She knew Sabrina was up to something, but just didn't know what.

Genesis office door opened, and the devil had dragged Sabrina in. She chuckled to herself, "Yeah. This bitch is up to something," and shook her head.

"So honey bunny, my cousin is here early and ready for her job interview." Sabrina cooed trying to seal the deal for her cousin.

Genesis rolled her eyes in the back of her head, "I told you I would interview her. I didn't guarantee you that I would give her the job. I hope that you didn't give her any false hope. She has to come in here, just like anybody else, just like any other job, and sell herself."

"I know that," Sabrina said with a slight attitude.

"If you knew that, then why are you up here during my interview time?" Genesis questioned.

"You know what? I'll just see you at home!" She was not going to entertain Genesis's attitude. Besides, she did have an agenda for getting her cousin the job. More free shit for her and her girls. She just hated that Genesis saw right through her.

She stormed out of the store, " I'll be in the car," she told her cousin Bobbie.

That was cool with her, she didn't ask the grimy bitch to come, anyways. She served her purpose for getting her the interview, now Bobbie could handle it on her own.

Chapter 4

Scolding her 4 year old son for having his toys all over the living room floor, she hurried to answer her door. Gasping for air, she peeked through her peephole, and shook her head in disbelief. His expression was not of a man that was happy, nor of a man who was there to kill her, but that was him. You never knew what was going on in his head. He could smack the shit out of you with a smile on his face.

All different types of emotions ran through her body with all types of outcomes running through her mind. Could this be her mind or somebody else playing tricks on her?

Her heart and body wanted to open the door, but her mind and what she did 4 years ago wanted to take her son and run out the back door. What she did was unforgettable, even if she was tricked. He had killed people for less than snitching. She didn't think she would be any different.

The doorbell rang again, as she was standing there, contemplating what to do next. One thing stayed in her head, "If this is him, how in the hell did he know where they were?"

The decision was no longer hers to make, as Nigel Jr. ran in to see who was at the door by looking out the window. "Daddy!" He screamed, and politely unlocked the lock his mother hesitated to unlock. She wasn't quick enough to stop him before she was face to face with her past, or possibly the future source of her son being motherless. She was face to face with death, well-dressed, smelling good, and looking good as hell with a killer smile spread across his face.

Once the door was opened, he charged at his father, jumping into his arms. Nigel King bear hugged his son as if it was his last day on earth. Tears welled up in his eyes. Feeling his son in his arms was bittersweet because he knew he still had to turn himself in to the authorities. There was no telling how long he would have to sit down for this murder and his so called death.

The death thing was a technicality. His lawyer can always say he fled the country because he feared for his life. The Duke thing could be considered self-defense. Duke did have his gun pointed at his sister, but then again, you never know what white justice was going to do to a Black man.

It did not take him long to find out that Teesha had moved to South Bend, Indiana, which was still in the Northwest region, just like Gary was. He stayed with his son and baby mama, until he got word that Sorrow was now being held for Duke's murder.

The little time he stayed there gave Teesha hope that they were going to be a family again. She was now going to be Mrs. Nigel King Sr., like she always wanted, before all of this happened, so she prepared herself for his return. She even moved to Gary to be closer to Nigel's family. Teesha kept seeing the niggas she was fucking with, but she kept her heart towards Nigel at all times and her child away from them. Her relationship with them was strictly for her sexual needs.

It struck her as odd when Nigel requested that Truth come get Jr. to come see him, or that Truth was the one to drop off money over the course of four years. She knew little about

Truth, but to Teesha, Truth could never be Nigel's type. Teesha was mixed with black and white, and she believed that black men had the best of both worlds with her. She looked white, but her body and her full lips said otherwise, so she felt her position was secured. Unless another mixed or white bitch came sniffing around, Teesha felt she had no worries.

That was back then, and seven years later. Nigel Jr. was 10 years old and Teesha now knows that King was not that type of black man. He did not discriminate, and just happened to like who he likes, when he likes them. Sitting at home, with a glass holding three shots of tequila, she is listening to her son go on and on about Se'maj, Truth and Nigel's little girl.

She hated hearing about their happiness, and seeing her son involved in that happiness. On top of that, he married the bitch, but she held it all in, partly because of her son, but mostly because of the money. With the help of liquor numbing her pain, she tried to be okay with everything.

Back in the day, Nigel was a whore, and she knew he was. She had caught him up plenty of times, so she tried every game in the book to tempt him, but he did not fall for it. In fact, Nigel start sending Truth's ass to pick up or drop off their son. Teesha felt Truth knew she kept trying to make advances towards her husband, but so what. She deserved to be with him because she had his child, not this bitch, at least not at that time. She had to find a way to get her life back and to get Nigel's ass away from Truth. Why couldn't he ever be faithful to her when they were together ? Why this bitch?

Chapter 5

Bobbie sashayed into Get'em Girls with six inch heels, weave tight, with a perfect, hourglass shaped figure. She was ready to open up the shop as usual. She had been working there for a couple of months now. She was business chic, as always, when working at Get'em Girl Creations. She purchased her gear from them just, so she could make sure they saw that she invested into them like they invested into her.

Sabrina almost messed up the whole thing, trying to be super thirsty. Bobbie had a plan, and it was going to take time to do it. She kept getting phone calls from this Det. dude. She avoided his phone calls, but for some reason, her dear cousin wanted her to at least hear the Det. out. She said he was talking 20 stacks.

Now, if she could find out who and where this Black Pantha character was, she could kill them and still get 20 stacks. She was down for it, but it had to be something simple and something that would get her closer to Black Pantha.

Sabrina better be talking about 20 stacks each, and her shady ass better not low ball her price just to add more to her stacks. Matter of fact, she would just have to go to the Det. herself, and not depend on Sabrina. Cousin or not, she knew that bitch loved a dollar more than she loved her damn self.

Bobbie set up the store for the first customers to arrive. She actually loved working at Get'em Girl, and hopefully, if she does this right, she would still be working here without anyone being the wiser. Genesis had already briefed her on the owners coming in today, and she was anxious.

Interrupting her thoughts, she watched as Alexus walked in. It was something about her ass she did not like, but she kept it cordial. The bitch has never done anything to her, so she wasn't going to treat her with any disdain she had felt for her. Alexus smiled at Bobbie and waved. Bobbie waved back and rolled her eyes when she turned her back to her, and kept doing what she was doing.

It seemed like every week, like clock work, Alexus would get a phone call, and she would go on break a second before she gets the call. She then goes outside to have the conversation. She always looked like she was up to something when she answered that phone. "Bitch better not get in my way," Bobbie thought as she watched her do the same sneaky shit today.

Chapter 6

Alexus had been working for Get'em Girl creations for well over 7 months now. She had been here 7 months, and she still hasn't met the owners yet. Since she was fired from her old job, she had downgraded as a sales clerk at a clothing store.

Alexus had gotten her nursing license revoked. She was accused of giving inmates prescription drugs to sell, which she was. She finessed those drugs from her second job at a Rehab facility. Coming up on her coins was always her main focus, but she thought she was too slick to be caught.

Alexus had been used by a lot of inmates, but she thought this inmate was different because he kept fucking with her the longest. He had stayed with her for 2 years at his stay in Indiana State Prison. Plus he was the one that encouraged her to finish her nursing degree and get a job as a nurse from the same facility. That was the longest any nigga stayed with her in or out of prison. She got caught doing a lot of shit for this man, and she found herself in a situation she couldn't allow to be seen, so she transferred without even contacting him again.

A couple of years later, once she transferred to Westville, in walks another inmate who she would risk it all for once again. The dick was good, and the money was good, as well. The difference between the inmates from Indiana State and the inmate from Westville is the one from Indiana State approached his women differently, he finessed them, made them feel like something and ultimately got what he wanted from them. He didn't lie to them or make their relationship out to be more than what it was he just did it suavely with respect just as long as they deserved it.

The dude from Westville he was blunt, to the point he didn't give a fuck how you felt either you was down or you wasn't, end of story. He wasn't saying any flowery words, and he wasn't stroking your ego, it was business with benefits and nothing more. He will cut a bitch off in a hot second if she wasn't acting right, if she wasn't bringing to the table what she was supposed to or if she was acting suspicious.

Same thing happened in Westville that happened in Indiana State except this time Alexus kept getting caught up, therefore she had to be removed and her mistakes in life came back to haunt her ending in her not being able to work as a RN.

So, here she was at Get'em Girl with one daughter and one son and no baby daddy for either. But, that all will change when her plan was executed. She felt like these niggas got out of prison and forgot about all that she did to hold them down, the fact that she had lost her job didn't seem to move them. But, everything would get better, after working in prison, her people were able to get her a job as a Nurse's Assistant in a Rehab/Psych facility.

Now here she was ready to blow the lid off of everything, not caring who she hurt in the process. Not caring how her revenge was going to play out.

While Alexus was deep in thought Genesis motions for her to come here, " By the end of the week Sorrow and Truth should be here to meet everyone that I've hired and everyone that is associated with the shop." Genesis told her.

"I've been looking forward to it,"
Alexus said with a genuine smile. She
went on about her day as usual except
for at her leisure she made her phone
call.

"In a couple of days she will be
here." she told the person on the end
of the other line.

"Good, remember what I told you,
you have to have something in common
with her to get her to pull you in
closer.

Alexus hung up the phone and contemplated what her next move would be. What would she use to get closer to this female? She chuckled to herself, She would use her childhood against her. The knowledge that she had about her childhood would solidify some type of solidarity amongst the two women.

Later that week

Alexus watched as Sorrow and Truth personified in their every move what a black business boss should act. If, she thought Genesis had her shit together these two women were on that level that she would never see herself.

Not because she couldn't be on that level but because her goals in life and agenda was different from those women who owned the shop.

If Lexus wasn't jealous before she was jealous now, it was one thing to know about your competition: the woman that you had lost to: it was another thing to see her in the flesh and to know and see that she was a bad mother fucker. Truth wasn't any slouch either, she was a bad bitch, and she would tell you so herself. But Sorrow, Sorrow had a gangster vibe to herself, not a new school rah rah but an old

Mafia type of vibe. It was like she knew what she was capable of, but she only used it when necessary.

When introduced to Sorrow and Truth Alexus humbled herself, she showed gratitude for her job, and she showed respect. Alexus took a liking to Sorrow, there was nothing ghetto in Sorrow's vocabulary, she spoke with knowledge and Alexus admire that. Knowing what she knew about her, she couldn't perceive how she turned out how she did and doing all that she had.

Nevertheless, Sorrow had something that she wanted, the life she wanted, and she had to do something to destroy it. She had to get Truth also she was Guilty By Association. She tended to get her revenge with the help of her friend, just a little while longer, and she can have every single thing her heart desires. She reasoned that she was doing this for her daughter and her son. So, fuck these bitches and whoever got in the way of her achieving what she came to do.

She was in a win-win situation, she was getting paid to do this, but she also had a chance to get something that she thought she lost, love.

Sorrow and Truth had different vibes about these females. When Sorrow looked at Bobbie she saw the masculinity in her, she wondered rather or not Genesis knew Bobbie was sporting an Adam's apple under that scarf around her neck. She didn't give two fucks about Bobbie being transgender but it was something to be said about a person that is disclosing their identity.

Alexus Seems to have a lot of hurt in her, she wanted something, she was desperate for something. Whatever it is she pray to God that they don't have anything to do with the shop or her. But, all in all Lexus was cool in her book she seemed to have good taste, and they seem to have the same taste.

Truth on the other hand radar went up on Alexus, she wasn't feeling her. She looked familiar but she couldn't place her face. But just as long as she did her job she wouldn't complain after all she was the help. Bobbie on the other hand she liked, she seems like somebody that she can hang out with. But again she was just a worker as well.

Both Truth and Sorrow knew that they had to have some type of vibe, positive vibe with these females. It had to be a level of respect between employer and employee. They really didn't know how Genesis was running the day-to-day operation. They didn't know how the protocol went or how she dealt with these two females. All they knew was that Genesis spoke highly of them, and they trusted Genesis. Plus from what they have seen on video camera Genesis would be right.

Chapter 7

The detective set back and read each file, he had entail on everybody even Bobbie. Bobbie was on something other than the other girls he knew each one of them had a reason to destroy the King's family. He will be damned if he continues to be a laughingstock of his Precinct. Of course, he has lost a lot of his sources since he was forced to retire as a Detective, So, his techniques of getting what he wanted was devious and unlawful.

Besides the new woman in his life had the same agenda as him, and he was going to do everything in his power to satisfy her every desire. Even if her hankering was blood he would make someone bleed, even if her desire was destruction he would destroy everything in his path and even if her desire went against the creed in which he took 30 years ago, he would grant her every wish and her every desire breaking his oath.

He already went against his oath by doing unlawful things to get the Kings and their little sister under the jail. Now, his plan was to either get them killed on the streets illegal or legally killed by the State.

Thomas Branson was in love, he was happy than he had ever been with his first wife. She was fair skinned , with a voluptuous body, high cheekbones, beautiful curly hair with reddish brown undertones and brown eyes. He never thought a woman that looked like her would ever be interested in him, but his beloved was, and he would do anything for her.

He met Beloved after he was forced to retire from the GPD and his pension ran out, which forced him to work as a guard at a Rehabilitation and Psych Center.

Thomas smiled to himself thinking back to when he first saw her, he never would have thought that he would be with a black woman, he had always fantasized about being with a black, but he never had the balls too. He never wanted the stares and the talk from his Catholic family. He grew up in a home where blacks were a synonym for everything bad. But, now that he has tarnished his name and lost everything he might as well go for broke and be with an African American woman.

The alluring vision of her came to him, when they were retraining her, it was his first day on the job, and she was giving them hell. He had heard several stories about this woman, her uppity attitude towards everyone.

There was a code red being issued throughout the facility, Thomas had just clocked in on his first day. Staff was running from different directions to one part of the cafeteria, where they were trying to sedate a woman who had evidently laid out a couple of nurses and another guard.

Her face was screwed up into an evil smirk as they tried to take her down, she locked eyes with Thomas just as they put the needle in her arm, she then winked at him and let the drug take its effect.

Every day since he had witnessed that incident she had an encore performance at least twice a week. It seemed to happen right when he clocked into relieve the other guard. It was as if she wanted him there but did not want him involved. It always ended with her finding his eyes with a sadistic smile and a wink.

He noticed that she would sleep for days after each episode, he knew what she was doing now. It was pitiful that no trained personnel uncovered her ruse. She wanted to be sedated, she was trying to sleep her time through, but she wasn't going to get out like that. He read her file, she came in addicted to heroin and crack cocaine. She had no visits from any family or friends.

They were the same in their aloneness , isolated and thrown to the vultures like dead carcasses. He would walk pass her room, to gaze into the small window at her. She was mostly sleep with her face covered but gazing upon her was his new-found addiction. Thomas had no idea why she was bewitching to him, she was beautiful yes, but the harshness of the drugs still showed on her face. Or maybe, it was harshness from something else that tried to cover her beauty.

One night he was walking past her room just to peek in and there she was standing right in front of the window waiting on his systematic walkthrough. Thomas stopped in his tracks, face turning a bright crimson at being caught looking in on her. Although, that was his job, e still let his feelings show on his face. She was more than a black dope fiend he was supposed to watch over. He did not even look at her as a dope fiend. Everybody in this world was addicted to something, it was just that some addictions were frowned upon in this society and others were embraced.

To Thomas's surprise she motioned for him to come in, she grabbed his hand and placed her hand in his as a dignified lady would have done to a gentleman caller. He obliged her request and placed a soft kiss on the back of her hand.

She uttered these words as she gazed into his eyes, "You can call me Beloved."

That was the end of Thomas's ability to resist the urge to protect her, defend her and conquer her every desire no matter what it was. Beloved had also done her homework on him and knew she would be able to effectuate her plan, her revenge.

94

Shaking himself out of his thoughts and focusing on the tasks at hand. Teesha would be an easier recruit than any of the other women, he knew Teesha was weak and gullible. He could tell by her phone conversations with her friends that she wanted to be and thought she should have been Nigel King's wife. Since she no longer feared for her life over the mistake of letting the cops get in her head and accusing Malakai for the killings of her cousins.

She would do anything for her and Nigel jr. to be the only family he had. Teesha was bitter over Truth and Nigel marrying and even more so after they had their baby girl she always wanted. She hated that he had another child, the Det. knew she would do anything to get what she wanted.

Chapter 8

Teesha knew when she got a call from a Detective it was not going to be good. All types of scenarios ran through her head. Why in the hell did a Det. want to see her or even want to talk to her? The first person she thought of was Nigel.

"Hey," She said as Nigel answered.

"What's up?" he questioned He always kept it strictly business with

Teesha's ass. He didn't even say remember the time to her ass, just to joke about something their son did while they were together. She would take it to whole other level. He didn't want her, and he wasn't trying to make her think otherwise. Teesha was the type of female that if you smiled at her too hard, she thought you wanted her ass, and she was willing to give anyone the time of day.

"Nothing, let me speak to Jr. right quick." Teesha said She hated that Nigel always got right to point, there was no bullshitting around, making small talk. The only in depth conversations they had was about Jr.

"He's gone with Tru and his sister." Nigel told her

"Oh, okay. Just tell him to call me, when he gets back."

"Will do." Nigel told her

She hung up the phone, well he answered the phone, so she knew he wasn't dead or in jail. She did not see any other reason as to why this Det. Branson would want to speak to her. Damn, she didn't even know rather or not Nigel was still in the streets. Nowadays, the only thing she knew about Nigel King came from their son.

Her heart was in her throat as the doorbell rang, she peeped through the peephole to this broad shoulder, actually attractive older white man with a crooked ass nose. He smiled, when she opened the door, "Miss Teesha Williams, I presume," he stated as he held out his hand.

"Yes," she said, shook his hand and led him into the house. She motioned towards the couch for him to have a seat, "Can you tell me what this is about?"

Det.Branson looked around and observed her home, "Where is your son?" he questioned her him last thing he wanted was witnesses to what he wanted to advise Teesha to do.

"Oh, he is spending time with his father before they go out of the country."

Teesha did not know it, but she had said something that would set his plan into motion immediately. Thomas went in for the kill, he had no time to play with any of these black bitches anyway.

"It's about a thorn in your side. Something that you have yearned for but you have too many people standing in your way." he told her as he reached inside of his briefcase,he then placed five pictures down on her table.

She was quiet the rest of the time he was there, if she was smart she should have been asking questions. But, she had tunnel vision and one thing that was on her mind was the hope that her prayers had been answered. She was down to do anything and everything to get what she wanted, even if it meant involving the innocent. Even if it meant taking away from her son, taking away the cushy life his father and his wife were providing for him, even if it came down to destroying her son's future to greatness. She would risk it to see if they both can have what they wanted. He took her only 20 minutes of deliberation to comply with his request.

She texted Branson, *I'm in*, it read as she set back and sipped on her wine and stalking Truth's Facebook page, Instagram, and her Twitter account. She kept looking at the pictures that Truth posted. You could tell her and Nigel were well off, in love and so forth by her pictures of them and her son. She wasn't hurting, but she wanted the type money she knew Truth had access to on a daily basis if she wanted to. She wondered how this pay out of a 100,000 thousand dollars was going to look on her. Good as hell she said smiling to herself, pouring her another glass and doming it as she held the glass bottle in her other hand. She was ready to refill her own damn glass.

Teesha was celebrating, celebrating the fact that she would now have more than this nigga's child, she would have Him and the money. She pranced around her home in her underwear, just as happy and drunk as she could be.

Now, this Det. Branson comes like the devil barring gifts, and she was ready to sell her soul to the devil to get her man back to get her what should have been hers. The plan was a little fucked up, but he ensured her nobody innocent would get hurt, and he could make sure that her name did not come up in anything. When they were done with it, she would be that familiar shoulder for Nigel to lean on.

Sabrina and the Det.

Sabrina was always happy when she saw "The babysitter" flash on her screen. She knew that it meant money, she was tired of her baby daddy giving a certain amount of money a month for his son and with Genesis trying to give her a damn allowance. The Det. was helping her get her own, her first assignment was to get Bobbie hired, she only got a stack from that, but she was promised 30'gs a piece if she could get her on board with this secret plan. But, Why the detective needed Bobbie in there she didn't know, only thing she was worried about is how much was he was willing to pay.

"What's up, Babysitter?" She chuckled in the phone.

"The plan goes down next week, they are going out of town, without their children. What makes it even better is they will be at your house for two weeks." he told her with happiness and eagerness in his voice. Just like Teesha,he stalked Truth's page as well.

Truth was one of those people who shared too much on social media, and he had found out that they wouldn't be bringing the none of their kids with them not just Nigel Jr. When she thanked G, for being a good Auntie and

Godmother for keeping them while they go on vacation.

"What the fuck?" Sabrina said in anger. She bit her bottom lip, not once did Genesis ever hint to or mention anything about keeping their kids, let alone a damn trip. She knew her and Genesis relationship was strained but damn she didn't even want to go on vacation with her. To her they were always forcing their kids on Genesis. Sabrina was so self absorbent you didn't even ask why he was so happy about the kids being left behind. She didn't hear his scheme but when she heard, "100,000 each," she started paying close attention.

"You can also get your relationship back with them out of the way, her loyalty would be to you. In your cousin's case she can get her revenge on Sorrow and her brother, for Jason." He preached.

"Like I said, you might have to meet with that thing!" she said with an attitude.

"It's been hard to get in contact with her." He admitted.

"Leave her a message, that would get her attention," Sabrina said rubbing her thumb across her fingers, like he could actually see her, indicating that money would most definitely get her cousin's consideration. "Money, then let the bitch know she can go ahead get her "snip snip" done." she said laughing hysterically.

Sabrina hated that she could not get her cousin on board for that extra 10 g's but now she was really pissed about not being able to get some out of her 100,000. But, her 100,000 wasn't anything to sneeze about. Damn, she thought what do I have do again for this 100,000?

"What do you want me to do?" Sabrina finally asked

The Det. smirked, these stupid black bitches better not fuck this shit up. "I need you to leave a door unlocked after you and your child leave."

Sabrina's face frowned up, "That's it?"

"Yep, that's it!" Det. Branson hung up the phone.

He turned to his Beloved, "These are some simple bitches!" he told her running his hands down his face out of frustration. She came up behind him to rub his shoulders, he relaxed as soon as he felt her touch.

"These bitches don't deserve 10,000 let alone 100,000 fucking dollars." he said shaking his head.

"What's four hundred thousand dollars to a million to get people to do your dirty work. You've been wanting to destroy them since the little bitch broke your nose. Besides, if Sorrow's team just so happens to find out who was involved, the only trail will lead to those stupid bitches. You got this, Big Daddy, your plan is going to work. " she told him placing a kiss on his neck. She had a sinister smile on her face as she walked towards the kitchen.

That was why she was his Beloved, as the blacks say, his ride or die. He thought to himself as he watched her walk away to go finish dinner. He knew it was something dark inside of his Beloved, why else would she encourage his idea involving children? Or was it hers?

He called Bobbie, "Snip,snip, 100,000," was the only thing he said on her voicemail.

He got a text, *When?*

I'll let you know when I get there.

"Damn, maybe the dyke bitch isn't stupid after all." he said to himself.

114

Chapter 9

Bobbie sat Indian style wondering what all she had to do for this 100,000 and would he be able to help her get her revenge from Jason's death. She knew what type of man Jason was, but she loved his dirty draws. She remembered when they first met; it was an attraction that had to be denied in the light of day.

Jason had a reputation that he wanted to uphold in the streets, and letting that type of attraction be known could ruin him before he could even make a big name for himself. That was also the reason she was even more attracted to him as the days, turned into months and finally 2 years, was the fact that he would do anything to succeed, and she found that quality in him breathtakingly naughty. Two years in close quarters brought Bobbie down to this bold move, besides Jason was giving off all types of hints.

Anytime she would pass him, he made sure to rub his dick or his hands across her ass. One night she noticed he would come to the showers when she did and while the others were all done. He would cut off the lights and shower; she kept an eye on him, that's what you had to do in a place like that anyway. Especially with a face, body and the type of lifestyle she had. She also noticed that each time they showered he got closer and closer until he was next to her showering.

It was pitch black except for a light glow from the office light. As she bent over to wash her legs and feet, she peeked through her legs to find Jason turned towards her jacking off, as he watched the soap run down the crack of her ass. That night she took a chance that many were sure would get killed by the hands of Jason. She jumped out her bunk, put the blanket around the bed to give them privacy, and she got her knees, undid Jason's pants and placed his penis in her mouth.

Jason kept his eyes closed at first, put then he grabbed a fist full of her long cornrows twisted it around his wrist, turned her head towards him, so he could look into her eyes and fuck the shit out of her mouth. After that, the relationship in secret grew from that and Bobbie was Jason's nigga, his ride or die.

Jason had got out of prison before Bobbie, so although Jason told her he had her just as long as she kept her mouth shut and stayed loyal. It was bullshit to her, until she got out and the first thing she went to have done was breast implants. Bobbie already looked like a very pretty girl, with a nice ass for being born a male.

So, when Jason wanted her to dress and act like a girl but keep her dick, she was all in for it, for her man that came through for her. Her homie, lover, thug was always honest about everything he did, even having sex with other people, male and female in order to gain the power he wanted.

The crazy thing was Jason always kept it kosher with her when it came to him fucking and killing his way to the top. He told her that he was going to do anything to run the streets and either she could go with the program, or she could get on with her life.

Now, all that was over and here she was a transvestite with no love of her life. She knows they said Duke killed him, but she wanted to know what were Sorrow's and this Black Pantha character's part in his murder. She had a feeling it was a lot more to the story, and she was going to find out. Soon.

Bobbie was not letting this Det. in her home, so she met him at the Library on 5th ave, in the parking lot.

She parked next to him backwards, she then crawled to the back seat where she left the window down, she kept looking straight. It didn't take him long to figure out that she wanted him to roll down his window.

"What I got to do?" Bobbie asked

"Get some of Jason's and Duke's friends, about two you can trust, somebody else will meet you there with her two. You go in and take Sorrow's son, advise your men to beat Genesis down. I don't give a fuck if you kill the bitch, she's irrelevant to our mission. We will have someone meet you at a designated place you will give the kids over to a female, you will know her when you see her. I'll keep in contact once the money come into play. " He instructed.

"When does my revenge come in?" she questioned thinking about how or what Jason would say in this situation.

"Don't worry, it will happen. " he reassured her, and he then rolled his window back up. Ending the conversation

Alexus

Alexus answered her phone, "It's time." she said

"What do you need me to do?" Alexus asked

"There is a plane ticket waiting for you at O'Hara Airport. I need you to get Malakai's phone he has a habit of leaving it in the car. Then I need you to make a phone call from his phone to a Nigel, he might have him in there as King. I want you to say what we have been rehearsing for the last 6 months, when we were in the facility. Don't you ever give them any indication of who you are. This is strictly business. Keep all your personal feelings to yourself until later. I will reward you with what you desire and 100,000." she instructed her.

"I understand," Alexus informed her, and she hung up. Beloved never knew about her involvement with Nigel King, that was something that she wanted to keep under wraps.

Chapter 10

Sabrina had awakened to Genesis already up, fixing her God children and Cameron some breakfast. Sabrina came up behind Genesis and gave her a kiss on the neck.

" Good morning, G". Sabrina said sweetly

"Morning," was all that Genesis could muster up to say to Sabrina. With the way Sabrina has been acting lately

Genesis would rather for her to be at her own crib instead of hers.

Sabrina overlooks the irritation behind her greeting. " I have to go drop Cameron off at his grandmother's, then I'll be back to help you with your God children."

Thank God Sabrina was smart enough to have Cameron sleep in his clothes, now all she has to do is put his shoes on and bounce. Sabrina tried not to look anxious as she was hurrying Cameron to put on his shoes. Once they were done Sabrina quickly went out the door, she kept her eyes off of the stairway above her and kept going downstairs hurriedly with her son in her arms.

Standing in the upper stairwell of the apartment complex six people dressed in black Timbs and black hoodies watched the redhead leave with her child, unfortunately the door to the apartment was ajar. Genesis had her back turned towards the sink washing dishes as the masked figures entered her apartment, The two who were not armed went straight for the children grabbing them up from the table. Genesis kept guns all over the house, with her background she never knew what would kick off. The four armed men tried to reach Genesis before she pulled out her gun.

However, in the quick motion of the kids being swept up behind her she already had yanked her gun out discharging it hitting one masked man in the head. She didn't have time to pull off another round because the remaining masked men were upon her beating her with pistols, their feet and hands.

The pain hit her immensely, with each hit that connected with her flesh, the sound of broken bones echoed inside her head the blows to her head were the most catastrophic feeling she had ever felt. She must have been relieved when she went into a comatose state. Her mind and body underwent complete darkness.

Haiti, Petionville

Truth, Malakai and Nigel decided to head out to Port- Au- Prince to do some sight seeing. Sorrow made the decision to stay behind to watch her Grandmother and Grandfather in action. Upon the death of their son the hierarchies decided to go back to the day-to-day operations, until they decided who was worthy enough to take over a 30-year reign of prestige and honor their family has held amongst their people in Haiti.

They were amongst several cartel families. But they were the only ones that bloodline originated from Haiti that are amongst the richest family in Haiti. Madsen, Brandt, Lacombe, Gardere, Mevs and Bigio were all legally rich, and they were not born and breed in the Island of Hispaniola.

It was a lot being discussed about the family history and the current situation around Sorrow in hopes that they will persuade her to take her father's place. Her grandmother Evelyn, she was Colombian, her father was the one who introduced her to Haiti and there she met her husband and stayed in Haiti. In 1964, she had her son, By 1985, the cartels began to seek additional transit points for cocaine coming to the United States. A natural candidate was the island country just south of the Bahamas — Haiti.

The number of Colombian narcotics traffickers residing in Haiti has been growing daily and the narcotics organizations are now using Haiti as a base of operations, storage site and staging area. In addition, these organizations are buying up legitimate businesses to serve as front companies for their smuggling operations. Once having gained access to local commerce, they then focus on corrupting public officials to protect their interests.

Evelyn and Ovince Jean-Baptiste was pulled in by her father and his ties to the Colombian underworld. Ovince had political ties and a was a Jeneral nan Lame ayisyen. Ovince being a General in the Haitian army sealed the deal for the Columbian drug lord, who brought his daughter along to stay in Haiti to keep an eye on things. The rest was history.

Haiti was a particularly appealing option for drug traffickers because of its location, its weak and corrupt government, and its unstable political situation. The Island of Hispaniola on which Haiti is located, is on the most direct route — barring transit of Cuba — from Colombia to the United States. Haiti has harbors and inlets which afford excellent protection to drug smuggling vessels. Moreover, the Haitian Air Force has no radar facilities and does not routinely patrol Haitian airspace. Drug planes can take off and land freely at any of the island's numerous secondary airstrips.

Priest Hunter Jean-Baptiste was in his 20s ready to learn any and everything he could about drug trafficking and more. He was a fair man but deadly if crossed. Going into the United States he made sure his credentials stated Priest Juste-Hunter instead of Priest Hunter Jean-Baptiste, better to confuse the authorities, his enemies but still have the men who did business recognize his credentials, if they questioned his caliber.

As Sorrow listened to her family quietly, taking in everything she wondered what her husband was doing at that moment.

At that moment Malakai was sitting in front of a window ready to eat his lunch. He placed his palms up to the heavens, and he blessed his food. Upon open his eyes just that quick he thought he saw a familiar female quickly walk pass. Then he noticed that a car alarm was going off, he patted his pants and his clothes to see if he had his phone because the alarm sounded familiar. He jumped up before Truth and Nigel came back, Better safe than sorry, He said to himself as he looked around as he got outside, the alarm sound was coming from the area his car was parked.

"Damn, mother fucker! He exclaimed as he saw his car window busted, his car had been rummaged through. He looked in his glove compartment to find his cellphone gone and the diamond encrusted platinum dog tags he had custom-made for his son. Nothing else was missing not even his stash of his money.

"Hey, Baby!" She said seeing his name plastered all over her screen always brought a smile to her spirit. "Surprise! Surprise! Surprise! I have your son, if you want him alive I would advise you to keep your wits about you and your cell on at all times. By the way your son's eyes are just as beautiful as yours!" The electronic voice assaulted her ears with this devastating news and it silenced her questions and homicidal promises she was about to throw at him.

Her heartbeat accelerated to a deadly pace, her eyes grew a dark shade of gray. How in the hell was she supposed to reach her husband if this mother fucker had his phone? Where the hell was he?

Just then her cell phone rung showing an unfamiliar number, she answered not saying a word. "Baby? Baby? Somebody busted the car windows and stole my cell." he yelled into the phone.

Just as Nigel and Truth came from their quicky in the bathroom, they noticed that Malakai was no longer sitting at the table, He was about call but then MG's name popped up on his cell, "What up, my nig?" He answered the phone!

"What up, Nigga?" the voice said. He looked at the phone at the number wondering why he was talking to a robot and not his boy, "Who the fuck is this?"

"You will find out in due time! But your main question should be, where the is your daughter? Keep calm mother fucker and your cell on at all times. I'll be in touch!" The electronic voice warned him.

Running out of the restaurant Nigel ran right into Malakai coming from a phone store next door. "I got a phone call saying somebody has my daughter."

"Are you fucking serious? I was trying to have a conversation with Sorrow but this janky ass cell phone not working right. Truth call Genesis. Somebody broke into my car and stolen my cell." Panic rushed the parents as they jumped into Malakai's vehicle hightailing it back to Gramme's. Nigel watched the tears run down his Wife's face as she said, "No, answer."

Nigel's heart ached, his throat became dry, his rage was building up at the news of Genesis not answering the phone. Maybe she's on the phone with Sorrow, he reasoned with a little bit of hope that this was just some kind of joke, he said a little prayer while speed dialing his sister!

He finally got a hold of her, "Somebody has my motherfucking child?" they said simultaneously.

Nigel had her on speakerphone, Malakai's heart accelerated hearing them, "What the fuccccccccccccck?" Malakai screamed pushing harder on the gas.

Truth hung her cell up from dialing Genesis for the tenth time, she balled herself up into the fetal position and started sobbing loudly .

"Did you get a hold of Genesis?" , Sorrow asked

"Hell no, Nigel said lighting a cigarette, nervously. "What did the person's voice sound like? Nigel questioned

"Fake ass robotic voice, Sorrow answered. Malakai started banging on the steering wheel, maneuvering through traffic as fast as he could. All he could envision was his son looking scared, being scared, crying for them. He prayed to God that it wasn't true.

"Call her ass again and call her bitch! Be there in 15 minutes." Malakai barked in anger. Nigel ended the call and prayed himself, through the cries of his wife.

Sorrow quickly dialed Genesis phone number repeatedly with no answer. She called Sabrina , and her phone went straight to voicemail. Sorrow paced the floor of her grandmother's Gingerbread mansion anxiously waiting for Nigel, Truth and Malakai to come from the city. She continuously paced back and forth praying, cursing and planning the death of whoever took Hunter and Se'maj.

Sorrows phone started vibrating indicating she had a text message, it reads," don't get anybody else involved in this matter, not the police and most definitely not your Haitian family. You will be hearing from me soon to give you further instructions. And sweet Sorrow I want every single demand executed exactly how I want it and when I want it or two sweet innocent angels will get sent to Heaven before their time.

Sorrow's grandmother knocked on her bedroom door. It was something in Evelyn's spirit that was nagging her about her granddaughter she knew in her heart something was going on with her, she was there to find out what.

"Nwa Bote, ki sa ki pwoblèm nan?" She spoke in her native language as softly and encouraging as only a grandmother could have spoken. (Black Beauty, what is the problem?)

"Yo gen yo vòlè li, pitit gason m 'ak nyès mwen, Granmè!" Sorrow not caring about telling her Haitian family, but she will obey the not calling the police request. (They have stolen my son and my niece, Grandmother.)

"Oh mwen Seyè, lanmò vin yo, lanmò vin tout fanmi yo." She quickly pressed her ring to signal for The Fidelite, before Sorrow could rush to her Grandmother to stop her, The Fidelite was their ready to strike. (Oh, Lord death came, death to their families.)

Sorrow's words stopped her from speaking, "Yo konnen sou Fanmi ayisyen m 'yo, she whispered in her ear. (They know about my Haitian Family.)

Hearing that her Grandmother told her loyal protectors, "Aksidan, eskize m ', ou ka ale sou jou ou." (Accident, excuse me, you can go on your day.) All turned to obey her orders except for one, who was her right-hand protector. He knew when Evelyn was downplaying her emotions.

"Explain, Evelyn said in English, she moved to sit down on the balcony of Sorrow's room.

Sorrow followed and explained to her what the text warned her not to do.

"Swa moun sa konnen ou byen oswa ou ap fè fas ak yon moun nan ki fè respekte lalwa." She warned Sorrow.

149

(Either people know you well or you are dealing with someone in Law enforcement.)

Sorrow took in what her Grandmother said, her mind was whirling with accusations as she nodded her head towards her in agreement.

"Nou menm domestik yo pral ede w pake ak jè prive a ap tann ou. Pwoteje m 'afiche, ou gen pawòl mwen, mwen pa pral entèfere sof si ou mande m'." She told her as she lifted herself off the chair. (Our servants will help you pack and the private jet will be waiting for you. Keep me posted, you have my words, I will not interfere unless you ask me.)

Sorrow fell into the embrace that her Grandmother was offering, "Mèsi poutèt ou, Granmè" was all she uttered.(Thank you , Grandmother)

Her Gramme' pulled off the ring that she signaled her army with. She placed it on Sorrow's finger, Sorrow was about to protest, "Don't worry, Black Beauty." She smiled as she touched her diamond studded earrings.

"Ou se pitit fi papa ou la." (You are your father's daughter.) She kissed Sorrow and left the room. She motioned for Domonic to follow her, she briefed him. They will hold back for as long as they can, Family is Family, and they will and have destroyed all in the name of Family.

Sorrow phone rang again without hesitation or looking to see who it was, she answered and was greeted with screams and panic "Sow, the babies are gone and Genesis is laying in a pool of blood. OH, MY GOD, I don't know what to do, I don't know what to do" she screamed

"Why didn't you call the police, Sabrina?" Sorrow questioned her.

"Cause, Y'all from the streets and that means no cops." Sabrina shot back.

"Yeah, but you're not?" Sorrow said to herself "Call the ambulance, under no circumstance do you tell them about the children, Just tell them exactly what you know about Genesis.

Sorrow felt like something was up, Sabrina was the type of bitch that would call the cops, even on her damn self. The little street knowledge she did have in her was from Genesis and damn near half of the east side niggas been in her back in the day. She was the type to react first instead of thinking, so analyzing the situation Sorrow knew it was more to what Sabrina was saying or what she was not saying.

Everybody's belongings were packed within thirty minutes, the private jet airplane was fueled a ready to go to fly them to the Gary Airport.

Chapter 11

Gunning the pavement towards home from the airport, every part of Sorrow was on fire, her flesh throbbed with a hatred you could only imagine the devil himself embracing. Her child gone. Her niece gone. One of her best friends were lying in a coma. Sorrow still hasn't went to see Genesis yet. The text updating her on Genesis's condition came when she was on the flight. Luckily, they had left their cars parked at the airport. Sorrow had sped off without getting her luggage or warning anyone about her abrupt departure.

The thunder roared greatly against the sound of rubber speeding through liquid, the rain punched down on the roof of the electric cobalt coated 2017 pitched forked adorned chrome grill Granturismo Sport, Maserati. Someone had the audacity to not just kidnap her niece but her son as well. Her fucking son!!! "Off with their motherfucking heads," she screamed beating the steering wheel with one hand and coxswaining it with the other.

Sorrow reached her destination within 45 minutes, in what should have

been an hour and fifteen minute ride,
if she was abiding by the laws of speed
limits. She already patronized the gas
stations in Gary to purchase a box of
Newports, along with a box of Swisher
Sweets. She was surprised she held it
together enough to get out of there,
because the way she was feeling, she
wanted to put bullets in the wind just
for blowing.

Securing the car in the garage,
she went directly into the basement
revealing a room with in a room full of
weapons, Kush, and a bar with a shit
load of monitors flooding the walls. A

wall that displayed TV screens securing every part of the house except the one she was in right now. TV screens with the visual of the Get'em Girl stores, Black Reign, as well as the house on the beach in Gary covered the others.

The day continues to thrive in slow motion as reality sets in; Sorrow hasn't touched a blunt or a glass of cognac since her reign as Black Pantha. Now, only now, has she craved the effect that the two would bring to her mental. She wasn't hoping for a taming effect, for it would take God himself to force her mental into serenity.

The potent smell entered her nostrils, while she sat Indian style surrounded by steel and pictures of her son, she could not smell the potency of the plant, and she only smelled the aroma of blood, the aroma of death. A smile crept upon her face, for she was the one creating the stench of demise, the fate she will bestow upon whoever took her man child.

Malakai knew this was a point of no return for her, as he watched his wife succumb to her dark side. No matter what he said or how many times he requested her to let him take care of it, he knew his protests were futile. So, instead of protesting once again, he walked downstairs to the basement, pushed the wall to enter the secret room, plopped on the floor next to his wife, grabbed the blunt and helped her load the tools that will orchestrate the return of their child.

Death and life formed around her ice-cold body inviting the wrath of Black Pantha, fuck the world she lived in now, fuck the leaves she turned over; somebody crushed those leaves and burnt them, with her own hellish fuel.

Inhaling the remains of those ashes, turned her eyes an ice steel gray, it furthered the evilness in her mind, as she saw what she had become die screaming and what she once was rise up out of fiery water with a devilish, manic grin plastered on her face.

The beast has been released, the majestic, deadly Black Pantha has come back to reclaim her throne and this time she was going to empty the clip or die trying. She knows she has the divine giving right to protect her offspring, and her family, and she was going to, by all cost. She will not lose another child.

Resurrection was the continued theme of the night, it was a deadly painful resurgence, nevertheless, it was a required one. Sorrow dared to be this person again, and she did not give a fuck who had any objections.

Someone or people wanted to belittle the sacredness of her son's life and her niece's by taken them for no reason. How was she supposed to get back what belonged to her, what GOD himself has honored her to receive, to birthed, to nurture, to raise, to mold into the greatness that Hunter King Gibson was created to be.

There wasn't even a ransom.

Why wasn't there a ransom?

Wasn't that what kidnappers did first, ask for ransom?

Someone had the balls to hinder the peace within her family and then didn't even put a price on it. That group of people or that someone did not know or has underestimated her ability to zone out into an inhumane state of mind. Chenille King had left her footprints in Sorrow's DNA, that combined with Priest Hunter's blood and her knowledge made her one deadly motherfucker to cross.

Now, was the time to analyze everyone around her, someone was connected somehow to her past and was now treading somewhere in her present manipulating her future. Could it be the bitches that got hired while she was out? Could it be Sabrina green-eyed jealous ass? Could it be someone from Duke Cash's family? Could it be someone in her inner circle? Or was it Karma telling her, her reign as Black Pantha was not justifiable enough with the divine order of things?

And this was payback for the blood she shed.

The lives she took.

The drugs she sold her own people.

Methodist Southlake

Sorrow's conversation with Rev. Walker was baffling, he had no idea Genesis was in the hospital. No one informed Genesis's family of what happened, no one contacted them about her current state. That did not sit right with Sorrow, there was no reason as to why Sabrina would not contact the Walkers at a time like this. Who in the hell would do some shit like this except a guilty mother fucker? Sorrow didn't care what part Sabrina played small or big, her life was at risk. Period.

Sorrow replayed the conversation she had with the Walker's had been so confusing. The conversation was heartbreaking. Sorrow confessed her thoughts to her husband. "You mean to tell me that, this bitch didn't tell G's parents?" Malakai asked in awe

"Dead ass baby, the conversation went like this verbatim." —

Hello, Rev, first let me say I am sorry about Genesis's condition and what happened to her. My family rushed from overseas to come see about her. We are here for whatever you need, Genesis is my sister." Sorrow let her words spill out so fast, she didn't hear the sobbing on the phone.

The Rev started sobbing as if it was the first time he had heard this information, the phone was dropped. Sorrow can hear some of her words being repeated. Mrs. Walker picked up the phone, "Sorrow, Baby! Where is my child?" she said with urgency.

Sorrow reluctantly told her best friend's Mom, "That's why I was calling you?"

She gasped for air, "Lord, please forgive me but If that green-eyed red bitch had something to do with this, I'm going to whoop her ass with bullets and ask for forgiveness later, Jesus."

"I will call around and call you back." she assured Genesis's mother.

Sorrow now was sitting in the parking lot watching for Sabrina to make her appearance. When she told the Walkers that she would call around, she went straight to Methodist Hospital in Merrillville when she found out where Genesis was located.

Chapter 12

Sorrow was dressed in an all black hooded jogging suit, hair in a bun and tucked in her purse was her trusty nine millimeter. This bitch could make a mother fucker tell on their Priest, literally. Sorrow commenced upstairs to where Genesis was, as she got closer to the room her footsteps got slower. She was frightened of what she would see once she entered the room. The squeak of her shoes against the freshly waxed floor made her stop in her tracks. She felt like the sound of her shoes added a loud disturbance to the quiet hum of the hospital.

The first thing she did was put her ear to the door, you could hear Sabrina talking in a very hush tone with the Doctor.

"Doctor, I know my wife did not want to be on a machine. I just don't know what to do?" She cried on his chest.

"The person's recovery depends on the cause and severity of the coma, unfortunately, anyone who falls into a comatose state is at risk of dying. In some cases, there may be a complete recovery with no loss of brain functioning, while in other cases, lifelong brain damage is the result. We are doing our best for Ms. Walker, Ms. Shepard." The Dr. placed his hand on her shoulder.

"I just thinking of her last wishes, Sabrina said shaking her head.

"You would be the better person to know what she wanted, seeming you are her only living loved one. We can have those papers drawn up, just in case. These decisions about whether and when to withdraw life support are not scientific decisions. It's really up to the loved ones of the patient." he confirmed.

"She was clear on not wanting to be in a coma or a vegetable. I want to honor her wishes." Sabrina said with candor.

Sorrow opened the door a little to see that Sabrina's back was to the door, she stood right behind her like a deadly cat, waiting. She couldn't really do anything to Sabrina at this moment, she had information that Sorrow needed and besides the Dr. would be a witness. Why bring an innocent into a war, if it was not necessary?

Sorrow adjusted her attention towards the hospital bed, there laid her best friend for over 15 years. Sabrina didn't adhere Sorrow's appearance until she walked up to the Hospital bed.

The tubes, the bandages, the swollenness, her dried up blood adorned her skin on top of bruises and open wounds. Sorrow's fist clenched, Sorrow's heart clenched. Sorrow's knees buckled when she saw that something else was breathing for her sister. After Sorrow gathered herself, she reached for her sister's hand.

While standing outside the door listening to Sabrina agree to kill her best friend she texted Lady Walker to tell her what Sabrina was trying to do. Sorrow then heard the door open, "My daughter did not want to have the damn plug pulled on her. She would want us to encourage her to fight for her fucking life." She looked right at Sabrina with ungodly eyes.

Sorrow stood with her back to the chaos behind her and focused on her sister, this was the G she would have never thought she would have to see. She reluctantly moved herself closer to her face, reluctant because she felt

the urge to lash out. The rage was
evident in her eyes, it was evident in
her spirit. This was dejavu'. This was
Genesis twin sister Gemini all over
again.

She reached G's ear, and she
whispered a quote, "Instead of a man of
peace and love, I have become a man of
violence and revenge." and she placed a
gentle kiss on her cheek.

Sorrow turned around and went into
the embrace of Ms. Walker and then Rev.
Walker as she walked past Sabrina, she
gave her a blank stare but locked eyes

with her. Sabrina made the mistake of standing completely still, she didn't even blink.

Sorrow learned that standing very still, may be a sign of the primitive neurological 'fight,' rather than the 'flight,' response, as the body positions and readies itself for possible confrontation, But, why would she be ready for a confrontation? Why would she fear her? Clearly she needed to be focused on Genesis's mother.

She kept walking keeping her eye contact with Sabrina, Sabrina was the one who broke eye contact before Sorrow hit the Hospital door. All she heard when she closed the door was" Bitch, how dare you? I'm calling the Authorities. Trying to kill my motherfucking baby."

Sorrow will deal with Sabrina sooner rather than later, she will get her answers one way or the other. She planned on doing just that tomorrow, right now she had a meeting to get to that was more important.

Sabrina

Sabrina felt the coldness rush against her back, but she just thought it was the temperature of the hospital. Now, sitting in her car, looking around clutching her mace, she knew that burst of coldness was the presence of Sorrow. How long was she standing there? Why didn't she say anything to her? Questions were running through her mind, questions only one person could answer for her and that was one bitch that she did not want to talk to.

"Yo, I just ran into Sorrow at the Hospital." She finally started driving, now that it seems like the coast is clear.

"Straight up! What did she say?" Bobbie questioned her

"Nigga, not a damn thing!" Sabrina said tensely

"What did you say?" Bobbie questioned

"She didn't say shit to me, so I didn't say shit to her."

"Are you serious bitch? Oh my God, dummy, how could have not over condolences or any type of help? You were the last person to she her children and Genesis. You just made yourself look suspect."

Bobbie was even thrown back by Sorrow's actions. She didn't know what to say to Sabrina.

"Real shit, Cuz, I don't know what to say. That was a dumb ass move on your part. Damn, that's some confusing shit. But, you need to stay available to look innocent or you need to call her and tell her your mind wasn't right. She's going to come see you sooner than later and you have to be ready with your story. We need to keep her guessing for as long as we can,

cousin. We need to get this money."
Bobbie reasoned with her

"You right I'm tripping! She
probably was just shocked to see G like
that. By the way Genesis parents showed
up and vetoed the plug pulling."
Sabrina said

"Damn, we just better hope she
doesn't wake up, until this is over."

"Yep, let me go!"

"Peace!"

Sabrina pulled out of the parking
lot of 555 Polk Street. She was so
terrified that she drove from the

hospital to the Police station. Now, Sabrina was about to pack up, her and her son and go visit her mother in Muncie.

Sabrina was not stupid, Bobbie did not know Sorrow like she knew Sorrow. It was not much, Genesis didn't speak up on Sorrow's business, unless it was something trivial. Come to think of it Genesis didn't speak about herself or none of their business unless it was something minor. Yeah, she was packing up and leaving because now that she thinks about it some of those hushed phone conversations were weird to her.

Sabrina went to her baby daddy's house to pick up her son, her shady ass didn't even warn him about what transpired at the hospital. As she made it home as she packed she asked herself, was money worth hurting or possibly killing the only person who treated her like something?

It was too late for her cold heart to thaw out, she was too far gone. Money had wrapped itself around her mind and was not letting it go. She could not hit delete on this one. She couldn't even lie to herself and say she did not know that Genesis was going to get hurt that bad.

She knew they were going to damn near stomp the life out of her or kill her. She knew it, and she didn't care at the time. Sabrina was all for it, she hungered for her own money, she did not want to keep living off of her lovers, welfare, and child support.

She put her son in the car, ran around to the trunk, threw the bags in, and ran into the car. Her hands started shaking thinking about the way Sorrow looked at her, she was trying her best to place the keys into the ignition. Something in her spirit felt danger, she started crying as she finally started up her car and pulled off.

"Momma, why are you scared?" Cameron asked

"Baby boy, I'm not scared. I'm just in a rush." Sabrina told him.

"Then why you crying. We can go to G's house. She told me no matter what she will always protect us because she loves us. Besides mom, I like it over at G's house than daddy's." Cameron said with a smile

The culpability was eating at her soul as she heard the love her son had for Genesis. In order for him to feel like that she had to show him love.

Sabrina had felt that Genesis didn't accept Cameron.

"No, baby boy! We are going to visit Grandma. Now it's a couple of hours, so we need to use the bathroom when we go to Mcdonalds."

"Yay" he rejoiced

Sabrina knew she was making the right decision, she did her part now all she needed to do was get paid. She didn't have to stay in The G, to do that, and she didn't have to wait for Sorrow to come get her ass either.

Chapter 13

Amongst the four parents hung an unspoken bond, the length of what they will do, did not stop short of their own demise. Since the kidnapper or kidnappers were just contacting Sorrow and Nigel they knew it had to be someone associated with them. But who? "

Malakai and Nigel had moved all their essentials from their house, in Illinois to the beach house in the

Miller section of Gary, Indiana. Truth and Nigel also will be staying a couple of nights in the house with them, everyone set up everything in silence. Everybody was in their own world contemplating -How in fuck did this happen? Why in the fuck did this happen? What in the fuck were they going to do to get their children back?

Truth was crying hysterically, "What if they kill them? What if they hurt my baby? Why did they do this? Why? Why?" she wept into a pillow while Nigel rubbed her back.

She was irritating Sorrow. Sorrow did not want to see that weakness in her friend and suddenly when Truth balled up into the fetal position, her cries echoed through the threads of Sorrow's throw pillows.

Sorrow finally, was the one to speak between the sobs of Truth, "We need to figure out who knew where the children would be? Who knew we would be out of the country? Which one of our enemies would do this? What is our first step?" Sorrow said as she looked upon the group.

Malakai," Sabrina's ass knew. And how many of those bitches at the shop knew?" He questioned.

"The only thing they knew was that we would be out of town. Unless, G mentioned she was keeping the kids to them herself." Sorrow said moving behind the bar. She started pouring everyone a drink, even Truth maybe that will calm her down. Sorrow thought in her head.

"Okay, what do we know about these females? Where did they come from? Who are they?" Nigel questioned his sister.

"I don't know. We just met them. Genesis did the hiring. Alexus has been working with the company for one year. Bobbie has worked with us for about 6 months. I have never seen or heard of neither of girls. Alexus seems quiet, but she's always on that damn phone. She answers that phone at the same time everyday, and she always made sure she has privacy. I don't know what is up with that but I will find out. Bobbie, it's something about her I don't like. Sabrina always has been a jealous ass bitch." Sorrow spilled out.

"So, basically everybody suspect that is in our visual every day." Nigel said

"Aside from what you and Malakai got going on?" Truth seemed to be able to say through her hysterics with a major attitude.

"How, MG and I make our money do not have shit to do with this. For one, I told you to mind your business. Second, we don't get in any business you and my sister got going on. we don't ask questions, we let y'all do y'all. Third, if you must know, we invested in this business secretly. We have nothing to do with the day to day operations. We deal in providing different locations for different events for secret stripper parties. Fourth, you wanted me to stay out of the drug and killing game. That is what I'm doing. But, right now you're thinking about the wrong shit." Nigel said while giving Truth the side eye.

196

Malakai peeked over at Sorrow and sure enough she gave him the blank stare, but he knew what the look meant. He knew what was in her head, *Since when do we keep secrets, Poochie?* This was about to be a long talk, but finding, buying or renting property for The XXX Underground Playgrounds was not illegal but it sure as hell was not legal.

They were trying their hand at real estate, buying houses and commercial buildings and fixing them up to rent or sell them to niggas in the hood. Nigel and Malakai knew their occupants or buyers were doing something felonious. They did not care about credit checks, background checks, they cared about the currency, the legacy they could leave behind.

Nigel and Malakai knew that they were well-known in the streets, being legends had its perks, let us just hope these young mother fuckers respected their gangster and wouldn't try any bullshit. Or was one of them little niggas behind this?

"Somebody could have been watching us, it's been 7 years since we've been in that life. But, still someone's from Pantha's reign could be behind this." Malakai admitted.

"What the fuck?" Sorrow said screwing up her face and looking at her husband. "So, I'm the reason why our kids were taken? We playing the blame game. Okay, Let's not forget about the infamous King Brothers and MG. Paid to bury! How many niggas have Truth finessed out of fucking money? Let's talk about that shit being the mother fucking reason."

"Control your tone, Pantha. MG told her in a harsh but calm voice, We are stating facts, fuck your feelings, Queen we need to get our kids back."

She knew he was right, he wasn't trying to attack her actions. But, deep down she was wondering the same thing. Could this be some sort of backlash from seven years ago? The carnage that she bestowed on her city seven years ago, was newsworthy. Her vindictiveness mania destroyed a lot of families including her's. She had lost one of her best friends, her father and a step-mother that gave her the motherly love that was lost to her as a child.

Seven years ago was a touchy subject for her, but everyone that was in this room benefited greatly from her actions, even though her husband was right, the next mother fucker that insinuated it was her indiscretions that put them here might just bring the Pantha out in her.

Sorrow lit the blunt she had rolled and took a couple of puffs off of it, this was not a puff, puff pass moment. She knew they were waiting for her to put it in rotation, but she did them one better and passed them all their own already rolled blunts with lighters. Sorrow knew the men would indulge in the Loud but Truth was a surprise.

Truth was not a smoker anymore, she hadn't hit a blunt in over seven years. But when she inhaled the smoke, she didn't choke or cough, not even a little. Sorrow's eyebrow raised, Nigel looked over at his sister, and then he stared at his wife. It wasn't that she was smoking, it was the fact that she was keeping it a secret. When she had no reason to, it made them assume she was keeping other things from them.

She smoked her whole blunt, when the other three only smoked half and put it out. Sorrow stopped wondering about Truth when her phone rung with a private number, her eyes widen with actual fear. Nigel and MG ran over to Sorrow, MG grabbed the phone and his wife hand at the same time. He put it on speaker.

The first thing they hear is crying in the background, the kids were crying for their mom and dad, they were crying for them. Sorrow's heart dropped, "Why in the fuck are they crying?" all three screamed into the phone. Sorrow's heart ached hearing them cry, but she refused to show weakness. She refused to let the tears fall, but having her child ripped from her, it felt as if she had awakened in that hospital room with her stomach empty. She was feeling that same rage build up inside of her. That same haunting feeling of being incomplete.

Reading from the paper his Beloved had given to him, his distorted voice said, "It's natural for children to cry for their parents, when they are amongst strangers. Your children are fine. My mission here is not to harm your children. But don't think I will not change my mind-"

Sorrow screamed into the phone, "Mother fucker, if you put your fucking hands on my kids-

The kidnapper ended the call

"Pantha, you need to calm your ass down. You don't think I want to curse this mother fucker out. You know how bad it's hurting me to bite my motherfucking tongue!" Nigel howled through clenched teeth, he slid his hands down his face out of frustration and turned his head to let the tears that was forming in his eyes fall. He just needed his daughter.

"This bitch forgetting her child is not the only one in danger. You can't be the fucking Boss of everrrything." Truth slurred.

Malakai embraced Sorrow and covered her mouth with his and bagged her away from everybody, he grabbed her face and looked into her eyes. He could see the fury in her eyes brewing into action. "Queen, focus on me, focus on getting our son back. These people have the upper hand on this situation. We have to be humble for now, we can lower ourselves for our son. We have to do what these people say until we get on the upper level."

Her phone rang in the distance, she walked quickly to the phone ready to swallow her pride, her brother kissed her on the cheek to let her know that everything was going to be alright. She placed the phone on speaker once again.

"I hope you had time to collect yourself and get your ego in check. Now, listen clearly and carefully. I already know with your background the authorities will not be involved. There are several missions that will have to be finished before you get your children back. The first mission, I want 500,000 each child." He waited

"We can get that to you within a couple of days." Nigel said, they had only half of that, but Nigel still had connections to get the other half. They had everything tied up in businesses. It was something too easy about this situation. Question is, "Why didn't they ask for the ransom up front?"

He laughed, "No my niggers, I want Sorrow to give me that Haitian money and I want the head cut off. I also want it visual to me, so I can make sure it's done. You have 5 days to get prepared. You will have a box sent to your business establishment, Sorrow. I will be in touch."

All of sudden Truth jumped up and quickly got in Sorrow's face. "You the reason why this is happening. All that mother fucking saying is Sorrow. Not Nigel, not Malakai and not Truth, but Sorrow. Sorrow steal and kill your fucking family. Yo ass wanted to sell drugs for that no hustling ass nigga. I told you to get stop messing with that fuckboy , Duke. Yo ass wanted to ki-"

Sorrow clenched her fist, but remembered this was her friend, so she quickly opened her hand up and raised it and smacked Truth so hard she stumbled into Nigel who was now standing right behind her.

Sorrow couldn't take it. She had to leave, she had to get away from her but first, she needed to remind Truth of who the fuck she is.

Truth held her face and looked shocked, mouth open, eyes wide open looking directly at Sorrow. Sorrow scowled at her, like bitch don't act like you don't know why you got smacked. As quickly as she thought it she opened her mouth to say it, " Mother fucker, don't act like you don't know why I fucking hit you! You are very fortunate it was opened handed. Cause I do not hit like a bitch. " Sorrow looked at her up and down with a snarling disgusting look and walked away.

Sorrow walked out on the terrace to clear her head, which turned into a walk on the beach. She touched her ring she placed on her right ring finger. She was not given things a second thought, she knew what she had to do and knew why she had to do it. The thing is how do you cut off the head, when the body was just as deadly. Was this karma? Question is who in the fuck would know about her Haitian roots?

Karma had come to her before she did something fucked up. Karma was on her ass in the womb, plotting, ready to destroy her with the very bitch that gave her life. Now, her choices as Black Pantha had led to the kidnapping of her children.

Bullshit, everyone who she dealt with, she dealt with accordingly, end of discussion. Her inner circle consist of her husband, brother, Truth and

Genesis, so she was sure they were out of the equation. Whoever was responsible better understand that Karma was not a colder bitch than she was.

Haiti

A smile crept on her face "Lage, Lage, Wa nan peyi etranje!"(War! War! King to foreign lands). The Fidelite started dismissing all the staff and all by five Loyalties were asked to go home or pack for traveling purposes.

Chapter 14

Bobbie and Alexus came to open up the shop, to find out they no longer were the first ones at the shop anymore. Sorrow, called the girls into the back through the intercom. Some girl they didn't know, didn't even acknowledge them as she walked briskly past them to let the rolling security gate back down. They both turned towards this tall girl, that look like she could be a sexy bouncer, then turned and look at each other. Both women thinking the other had done something wrong, like stealing money and, or clothes.

Alexus's mind wondered did she take it too far, walking past the restaurant was not in the deal. She wanted to see if MG would run out of the eatery and hunt her down, calling her name, just only getting a glimpse of her flowing dark hair as it turned the corner. Then she would disappear into thin air. Leaving him with images and yearnings for her that would consume him into coming to find her, and then she would do what she needs to do to get him. That never happened, he never left his seat. He looked up once

215

and then a second time, downplaying her moment with a nonchalant look that said, Oh is that?

Bobbie tried to research her mind about that night, she was masked, the usual all black hood attire for doing dirt, the black hoodie and black pants. The other person was dressed the same, Bobbie didn't even know who she was. Where could the slip up be? A couple of seconds went by and it jerked her into a halt. She pulled out her phone, and hit three on her speed dial.

Busy signal.

Three again.

Busy Signal.

Three again. Ring." This
subscriber is no longer accepting
calls."

What the fuck? What the fuck?
Bobbie's heartbeat accelerated. Did
this bitch get a case of the conscious?
Damn, she screamed in her head. These
bitches are going to kill me. These
bitches. OH MY GOD, I took their
children. I knew Sabrina couldn't
handle this shit. Wait until I get a
hold of this bitch, Sabrina. She
continued walking, strutting slowly as
if she hasn't done anything. But, she
looked back at the pretty but burly
female, that stood by the stores exit
door.

She could take a chance with this
big bitch, and just jet for it, then
she still would have to deal with it
later. Glancing over at Alexus, Bobbie
twisted her lips, Look at this bitch.
Looking scared, what the fuck did she
do let her friends go on a shopping
spree? Please, God, let this Latina
bitch be a thief. When I get this
money, God. After, the surgery. I
promise the rest is yours. She was
praying and begging so hard, her balls
were sweating.

Both women reached the door at the
same time, they put on their game
faces, they both acted like it was any
other day.

All smiles.

All Good.

They walked in, Sorrow was just hanging up the phone with a puzzled look on her face. She was extremely pissed off, she wasn't trying to show it, but just a second of a weak moment can show up in any gesture or facial expression.

Sorrow was pissed off at herself for allowing that bitch Sabrina to leave, now all sudden her ass was gone in the wind. She turned around to Ghost and Truth, "This bitch Sabrina is suspect. At, first her number was busy, now it's disconnected."

Ghost nodded her head.

"I'll text you the information."

Ghost headed out the door.

"Take Cabrera with you."

Ghost closed the door behind her and locked it. You can hear the click sound echoing throughout the room. Alexus jumped just a little at the sound. Her and Bobbie both seemed uneasy about the door being locked. Why would the door need to be locked? The silence felt like the calm before the storm.

"Good Morning, Ladies. Sorrow and Truth chimed in together, their voices did not reveal anything.

Truth started off, "We would like to speak with you individually. Bobbie you will stay with me in my office."

Sorrow just looked at Alexus and walked into the open door of her office, Alexus had never been in this office, this door had remained locked. Genesis never discussed with them what was behind this door or why it was locked, and they never asked her. Automatically, Alexus felt a little envious of her Boss's office.

"Close the door, Sorrow instructed her. She smiled as much as she could as she obeyed the command, have a seat."

"Genesis, is in a comma. " Sorrow watched Alexus expression it was one of shock and concern.

"I'm sorry to hear that, Genesis told me you three has been friends since Elementary. Do they know why this happened? How long she will be in the coma?"

Sorrow was looking directly at her with no expression on her face, "I'm not at liberty to say. The reason behind me giving you that information was to give you some type of indications as to why Truth and I are taking back over the day to day operations." Sorrow gave her a small smile.

"Oh, okay! Well, I hope that she comes out of it. Sabrina must be going loco?" Sorrow made a face at the mentioning of Sabrina's name. She continued, Then again probably not, she seemed to me that she sell her cooch to the highest bidder or the lowest." Alexus gave her uneasy smile.

Sorrow chuckled.

Alexus went further. "Did you grow up with her, too?"

"Naw! Thank God!" Sorrow admitted while shaking her head.

"Well, I'm glad you had a childhood you can share with your friends. I was the one who was locked up with mother monster." Alexus told her.

"That's unfortunate!" Sorrow told her.

"Yeah, When Genesis and I were having lunch. She mentioned you had a similar story to me, said we would have a lot in common. Yeah, she told me the story of your mom leaving you out in the cold and a neighbor lady used to take you in until your stepfather came home. I love that story, it takes a village right?" Thinking she had just won the confidant of the Boss she sat back and smiled.

"Who-her cell phone interrupted her from telling Alexus off.

Alexus sense the look on her face was not that of a person that was impressed. While, Sorrow's back was turned she exited. Scolding herself for being overzealous, she ran into Truth, "I have an emergency at home, my son has been rushed to the hospital." She told Truth in a rush before Sorrow could even make it to the front to interrogate her. Alexus was gone.

Just like that Sorrow knew something was up with this bitch.

Alexus did not get too far Ghost and Carmen were just pulling up, when Alexus hightailed it out of the shop. They both jumped back in the car and followed her to her destination. That was the other reason Sorrow sent them out there. Anybody who fled was to be followed, Ghost and Carmen did just that.

"Is that?, Ghost questioned

"Si! Carmen confirmed while frowning. The gentleman hugged Alexus, and she invited him in her house.

"Innocent!" Ghost looked at Carmen.

"Innocent until proven guilty." Carmen countered.

They brought the information back to Sorrow with a heavy heart. The look on Sorrow's face was undeniable, her stone poker face was in shock and full of questions.

Sorrow was going to have to scrutinize this situation herself. First, she was going to have to go to the hood and do a round up. Sorrow didn't utter a word to Carmen and Ghost, she removed herself from her office, got in her car. She drove down the block, no music invaded her background. Only thoughts, only violence, and only her son were the sounds bouncing off of her vehicle walls. She had a gut feeling Alexus was playing a part in it. Sorrow pulled down an alley on Broadway, she kept her engine running, she stretched out her arm to turn the radio on full volume.

She screamed.

What the fuck was he doing there?

She bellowed out obscenities.

Who the fuck was this bitch?

She shrilled out homicidal thoughts like a murderous banshee.

Sorrow assaulted her steering wheel, she mauled the face of the person who might be betraying her and the bitch he was disloyal to her with. Her frustration was out, her mind and to follow her back to what really mattered and that was her son. Haiti was the first step to getting him home. No sidetracking or sideline hos will hinder her mind from her son.

Chapter 15

Lord, though there are enemies who may seek to do mischief against the team – You are God! You cover us! You will protect us and bring confusion to the enemy camp!!! And we – the upright – shall dwell in Your presence!

Haiti

Once they landed on her family's' land, they were geared up, ready, to take down the men who were guarding her grandmother and grandfather.

Sorrow did not see this coming, one on one, there were two different generations of powerful women, one had already spent her life doing anything she had to for her family good or bad, wrong or right, Godly or devilishly, not one regret crossed her mind, and no regrets ever will. The other woman had spent a big part of her life struggling and surviving hate, poverty, abandonment, betrayal, abuse and all before she even bled like a woman. For the men she loved and the women she did cherish she killed for, she sold drugs for, she did things all in the name of love she wouldn't do for herself. Some betrayed her some stayed true. One thing remained true of both of these women is that loyalty reigned supreme in character and if that was not in your character, they didn't need you dirtying up their caliber.

"Where the fuck is everybody?" MG observed.

The Gingerbread style Mansion looked as if an ancestry of slaves were going to run out amongst their graves from the dark, isolated structure. Felt like howls and moans were reaching out to them to give them background music to their wrong doing. Sorrow has never felt any conflicts about killing anyone until she was told she would have to do this, basically kill and demolished her family, a piece of her, she would not be here if it was not for this woman and this man, and the people who created them. Here she was their flesh and blood, their bloodline on their land ready to destroy them and their legacy.

"Naw, this is war baby! We are going to have to work for this either now or later." Sorrow looked at her husband, pulling out two .44 AutoMag pistol from her fatigues.

Malakai looked at Nigel, Nigel shrugged his shoulders, he trusted his sister with his life. He was going to follow her lead and ask questions later if needed be. Nigel grabbed his AK 47, and aimed ready for anything to move in that house. He wanted his daughter back, he wanted his nephew back, so whatever sick shit this motherfucker wanted them to do, they would have to do.

MG, was ready to follow his wife, he too trusted her, but he sometimes knew his wife kept secrets, shit she does not tell a soul until the time is right. He knew she meant well but-

"Don't mention Ovince in any way shape or form. I shoot, you cover me." Sorrow commanded. When she would say shit like that, he knew it was more to the story. Malakai said in his head.

"Turn on your mics and cameras let's give this trifling ass hunky what he wants." Nigel said

"How do you know he's white?" Ghosts said sitting in the green Army van.

In unison, they all said with conviction, "because he says NIGGERS, Ghost!"

"Oh, yeah that motherfucker is white and a racist, I can't wait to kill that son of a bitch." Ghost told them over the running van.

"Ghost, look at your people! Maldito triquillo Gringo." she said jokingly.

"Mierda estúpido. Ghost said. Sorrow shook her head slightly while lifting her hands for them to turn on their cameras and microphones, and she proceeded to the front, she signals for MG to go to her left and Nigel to go to her right.

They entered from three different ways each going as cautiously as they could, slowly showing their guns before showing themselves. Nigel and Malakai had long corridors to come down, both men opened the doors cautiously one by one. Sorrow went straight towards the great room both guns ready to riddle bullets in anything that moved.

"Let me get my popcorn!" the man says excitedly in Sorrow's ear. Sorrow rolled her eyes, bullets whizzed by her head, dropping to the ground, quickly moving behind the couch, she glanced around it to find one of the soldiers. She laid flat on the floor. The soldier's leg was visible, she aimed, fired the bullet into his leg, he dropped instantly. She reached on her waist and pulled out another gun, shooting several more times. She placed the gun back in her waistband and picked the other gun that she put on the floor up.

More bullets, each entering the couch. Sorrow crawled Military style to the other side, jumping up to find one huge mother fucker shooting at her, in the darkness she could see how far up the fire was shooting out the gun. He was still shooting at the spot as she aimed and entered several bullets into him. Thud! The doorway popped open. Pow. Pow. Thud. Thud.

Nigel heard the gunshots, he had entered a room he couldn't get out of, the door was stuck, he ran to the windows. No. He ran back to the door. More gunshots. He aimed his gun at the lock on the door. Pow, pow,pow, bing, bing, bing, the bullets bounced off of the door. What the hell? He threw the vase off the table, picked up the coffee table and slammed it against the window. The window didn't even groan. What the fuck?

He was stuck.

He was livid.

He was panicking.

What was going on with his sister? What the fuck was going on with this house? He was hoping that those lessons at the abandoned warehouse was sufficient. It was killing him not to be out there. The not knowing, made him more determined to get out of the room.

Malakai shuffled into the room with his guns drawn, mind was whirling in different directions. Something was wrong with this situation. Giving the legacy and the thought process of the Jean-Baptiste family, that he was schooled about and absorbed by working for Hunter, was that war meant you never let the enemy past the palace walls.

They were behind the palace wall without so much as a soldier in sight.

He shook his head as he closed the door behind him and went further into the room. He looked around in the darkness, Sorrow must have forgotten he introduced her to her father.

Shots. Adrenaline kicked in Malakai ran to the door, turning on the knob, something was hindering it from turning.

More shots.

Damn His wife!

His Queen.

Panic. Yanking the door handle. Same results.

He ran his hand over his face, calming himself.

He took his gun, paraded bullets around the whole door. The door broke and fell outward towards the hall. Quickly he ran out, just as King was running out the door down the other hall. Guns in hands running towards the same destination. Their feet stopped, before them was a room decorated by bullet holes and shredded furniture. The marble floor was adorned with five dead Haitians. They searched the room for Sorrow, she was no longer there, but she left the trail of her presence in the form of blood all around that sitting room, like fresh red paint leaving the finishing touches on the newly decorated room.

Nigel nudged Malakai drawing his attention to the open door. Quietly they walked to the door, guns lifted, ears looking for sound of voices.

The Kidnappers

On the other side of the camera Branson and Beloved looked on in excitement, Beloved had no expression on her face, yet Branson was enthralled in every move Sorrow made. The dancing of his eyes as Sorrow ministered death upon these militant killers was a disturbing sight to witness. Beloved felt the missions was not over until she killed the head, she was not impressed by her killing men, she had no ties to.

Beloved wanted to see the finale, she wanted to see if she could steal from her own family and that she could kill the last elder of her bloodline. They watched on waiting and salivating over the ending when Sorrow would secure that bag.

Haiti

The men entered another room with no furniture and a plethora of candles were lit adorning the walls, tables, floors and there stood Sorrow above her grandmother.

Evelyn was gracefully and beautifully sitting Indian style, dressed in all white, black thick hair parted down the middle draping to her waistline. Her palms facing the sky, eyes closed and her voice soothingly leading her death with prayer.

Sorrow did not utter one word but reached below her feet with a flick of the wrist she twirled a Haitian

Machete, like she has been fencing with it her whole life.

Evelyn's eyes came up and landed on Sorrow with a blank stare, "Zanbi!Zanbi!," she arose from her sitting position and stood. She stared at one spot chanting as her granddaughter readied herself, readied herself to get back her son. Readied herself to be disgusted in her own skin. Readied herself to hear her father's screams of agony beyond the grave.

Readied herself. Raised it above her head.

Readied herself. Ready. Please forgive me.

In a trance, she pictured her son, and she brought that blade down smoothly to her Grandmother's neck. Machete was sharp enough to slice through flesh and bone and with one swipe, the blood of her Gramme' spray painted the room walls, dripped on the floor, squirted the candles and it's flames with crimson. Sorrow caught the head in her hand, she did not cringe at the sight. She looked pass to the mirrored wall at her image. She had a divine given right to protect her offspring. She was a Black Pantha.

The men looked on in awe. They couldn't look on as she held the head. No words were needed. No words could have been uttered.

Black Pantha does not notice the blood dripping from her grandmother's severed head that she held against her bosom with her right arm, nor the blood drenched machete she held tightly in her left hand. Her mind was focused on her Gramme's body that had not yet fallen to the ground, her body had not yet brought her even to her knees. It stood there as if the head was still attached, as if the blood was not spraying and pouring from the opening.

She looked down at the grotesquely beautiful detached head of the great Evelyn Cazador Jean-Baptiste and fell to her knees as she stared into the eyes' of her Gramme', she reached over to close them as she did the body then fell to its knees and collapsed before her. Sorrow wanted to weep but Black Pantha did not have time for weakness not when it came to her offspring, she would take a machete to her own head to save him.

Her loyalty was to her son and niece, the innocent, she then took the microscopic camera off her army fatigues and held it up so whoever was looking can she her eyes. They were grayish black, illuminated with darkness and loathe for whoever was behind this demented game.

Black Pantha gritted her teeth as she snarled out, "This will be you mother fucker, (she held up her gramme's severed head) if my babies have so much as the fucking sniffles when I see you." She then spit in the camera, threw it to the ground and crushed it.

Laughter erupted but the sound of worry was evident in his voice when he spoke, "This sick bitch actually, did it, he turned around to the audience behind him, I can't believe she did that shit."

"I can, the person said. Doubt crept in their mind, who knew the little black bitch had balls. She was unfamiliar with the unsavory things a mother would do for her children. Secretly she admired her for that and at the same time it also fueled her hate.

Chapter 16

Sorrow was riding in the car with Truth, in her head she analyzed MG, the MG she knows, knew when he was being followed. He knew she was following him now. But, how long has he known she had been following him?

"You think he knows?" Truth asked

Sorrow squinted her eyes at Malakai's car, "That nigga know!" She attested. Sorrow's mental could be described as a hurricane of thoughts. What's the reason behind this shit? She was mostly mad she had to deal with this while trying to get their son back.

Once Sorrow knew where he was going, "It's a bar up the street, I'm hungry." Sorrow pointed down the street.

"What the hell?" Truth said

"I don't have to give you an explanation on everything that is going on in my head. I'm hungry and it's a bar up the street." Sorrow said nonchalantly.

Truth did not know exactly what was going on, but if Truth was not letting the drugs take over her state of mind, she would have known exactly what was going on. Why did she not know her best friend, anymore? Truth didn't even know herself anymore.

Sorrow pulled out her Tablet, while sitting down looking at the menu. Truth once again was left to wait until Sorrow made the move, what was her next call as she typed away and maneuvered her screen. Very nonchalantly. Almost as if she was taking the time to do something so simple, so everyday-ish. It was as if, what brought them to this point was not devastating and life altering.

The waitress arrived with one menu, "Crab cakes and a bottle of your Pinot Blanc? She asked Sorrow.

"Please and thank you." Sorrow smiled

"We're going to share, Truth said declining the menu the waitress was offering her.

Sorrow was aware of Truth's bewildered look, she knows what she was thinking. They haven't spoken about the incident, they both decided without words to focus on getting their children back.

She handed Truth the tablet and her headphones. Seven small boxes of someone's house was on the screen. Her eyes became big and her head jerked up at Sorrow in disbelieve. Sorrow kept eating and drinking.

"How long have you been following him? Why would you be following him?" Truth asked wondering did this have something to do with the children being kidnapped.

"That day she disappeared from the shop, she was followed. The address she gave Genesis on her application was not the same place that she was followed too. That raised a red flag, so from that day forward she has been watched. Then one day I get a video sent to me of my husband pulling up to that same house. First couple of times I sent the girls, he was knocking on the door at the beginning, or she would arrive to open the door," Sorrow stops, gulps down her glass of Pinot and pours herself another one. She continues, "Then after a couple of weeks this mother fucker starts using a key to open up her door. I'm pretty sure you can figure out the rest." She gulps down her freshly poured glass.

"Damn, he's fucking her." Truth said surprised at seeing the girl go down on Malakai.

"After all that, you're surprised at what you see before you. Let's go."

Arriving at the door she quietly entered the house with the copied key, she decided to pull her hat down to cover her eyes and advised Truth to do the same. Sorrow knew the little boy was still in the house. No need for unnecessary dead witnesses.

Sorrow crept in the bedroom, the light flickered off of her husband's chocolate chiseled body, his eyes were closed, one hand was on the bedpost and the other was holding his dick and there in front of her husband, worshiping her dick, tasting her dick, gagging off of her dick was Alexus.

Kneeling before her husband as if it was her place to do so.

Sorrow steps closer.

Engulfing her husband's manhood in her mouth as if it belonged there.

Sorrow steps even closer.

Inhaling her husband's arousing scent was this bitch.

Sorrow was close enough to lean in without disturbing Alexus from doing her blow job. Sorrow placed a hand in Alexus hair, reached in and licked her husband's lips as she yanked Alexus

261

backwards and off of her husband's penis.

The pain hit Malakai, and he swung first, then his eyes popped open. "Sorrow, he screamed once his vision was clear. His fist connected with Sorrow's lip.

Alexus was too intoxicated to realize what had happened, " How dare you call me that,Bitch's name!" she slurred.

Sorrow laughed hysterically," Bitch, as if he would ever make that mistake." she wiped the blood off of her mouth and stared at her husband.

Malakai pulled his pants up as Alexus stared at the two women standing in her bedroom holding her and her man at gunpoint.

Fear of the unknown surfaced on Alexus's face, she did not utter a word. She knew who Sorrow was, the wife of her man. She had rekindled her relationship with Malakai too soon.

What would Beloved say?

What would she do to her?

The taste of blood appeared on her now busted lip, the taste of her own blood always sent a message to the beast inside of her to arrive, to get lit, a calm washed over her as the evilness in her eyes fixed their vision on the man who she thought loved her. Sorrow erupted in laughter, hysterical laughter of disbelief, sinister laughter, that said: "This nigga must have forgotten who the fuck I was." Still calm, no words were uttered as she pulled out her nine millimeter, took it off the safety, cocked it and aimed it directly at Malakai.

He was stunned and speechless, he knew no amount of sorries would correct this, he had a reason why he struck her but right now this shit looked all bad. Sorrow waved the gun back and forward from Malakai and this naked ass bitch with a Family Dollar bra and panty set on.

Sorrow nostrils flared and her lip curled upward, she swung the gun at Malakai and said with laughter, "This bitch got on a fucking Family Dollar bra and panty set. You see this shit Truth? You fucking a below standard ass bitch. Mother fucker you hit me over this bitch. You chose this I'm fucking all the inmates in Indiana ass Whore over ME! What part of the game is this? You ruined a good ass marriage for this, for this I'm for Everybody ass bitch. Nigga, you have the audacity to do this now. NOW, MY NIGGA. No mother fucking loyalty. It's OK. It's cool I know when I'm defeated." Sorrow laughed, "You know what song just popped into my head, and she started bobbing her head to the beat that was in her head. She started singing, " Nigga don't believe that song, that niggas wrong. Gangstas don't live that long." Still, with the gun aimed at Malakai Sorrow pulled the trigger. POW!

The girl screamed as Malakai fell to the ground. "Oh, don't worry baby girl I got 15 left with your name on it. But, first, take off that cheap ass shit. You could have at least went to Citi Trends. Second, you are going to tell me what the fuck you know about my son or I'm just going to kill yours. Third, who in the fuck sent you or is this just some woman scorned type of shit. " Sorrow laughed psychotically.

"Look, I'm sorry about your son but, I do not know anything about your son. I have a son, I would not wish for my son's brother to be kidnapped." Inside Alexus felt a little satisfaction from spilling that tea.

Sorrow did not blink an eye or show any emotion, she walked towards Alexus with her gun aiming it directly at her. Fear came in the form of liquid running down Alexus's leg. Sorrow smirked, "Ever heard of DNA test first bitch." She smacked Alexus's with her gun knocking her unconscious.

Truth pulled Sorrow to the side, "I knew that bitch looked familiar, that bitch used to fuck with your brother when he was caged in Westville. He pointed her out as she was passing by one visit."

"So, this bitch was fucking around with both of them. The question is, who did she come for Malakai or Nigel? I don't give a fuck whose son he is, if the mother had something to do with kidnapping our children, Sorrow's laughs, All I have to say is an eye for an eye is in the bible." Sorrow turned around and walked out the house. She texted Carmen and Ghost, *Dig deep and dig hard on anything to do with Alexus, ASAP.*

Truth cringed at the thought of killing a child. Sorrow has been taken to the point of being inhuman. Truth knew Black Pantha was in control and Sorrow was somewhere buried deep within her. Motherfuckers were in trouble, let's just hope innocent blood does not get shed.

Truth followed her out , "What did you shoot MG with?" She knew Sorrow shot him in the leg. But shooting him in the leg was not going to knock his ass out.

"A sedative!" Sorrow chuckled

After, Sorrow left MG on the floor knocked the fuck outm she went straight home. Truth retired to the guest wing of the house and she venture off to her and Malakai's side of the house.

Sorrow's phone vibrated, she answered.

"I want whatever narcotics you confiscated from the premises to be switched with some drugs in the evidence room. I have certain dealers I want you to shop your product too. But, in order for you to get those names, you are going to have to hack into the law enforcement files to find their territory. I will contact you at a later date to deliver my money. I don't have to remind you what is at stake, if these demands are not met or if I feel as if my life is in danger." The call ended.

Sorrow peeled her clothes off, felt the vibration of her phone again. Malakai. She didn't answer. She grabbed a bottle of Hennessey, a blunt and turned on the shower. Her tears flowed, the Hennessey was gulped the blunt was hit and the anger was fueled. Half the bottle gone and the blunt gone, she stumbled out of the shower into her walk in closet and selected an all white cotton sundress.

Thunder shook the house, dark clouds gathered outside. She peered out the window and smiled at the rolling dark clouds and the strike of light hitting the sky. God was setting the atmosphere for her pity party.

Her phone rung.

Malakai 20 missed calls.

Nigel 15 missed calls.

Truth 10 missed calls.

"Damn, she screamed at her cell phone, "Can't you get the hint I don't want to fucking bothered!"

Ring. Truth. Reject.

Truth texted her after being rejected, it read, MG told Nigel what went down and they are trying to get a hold of you. I told them you would talk when you are ready. love you , call me if you need me.

Ring. Malakai. Reject.

Ring. Nigel. Reject.

Maybe now they will get the hint.

Sorrow kept rejecting everyone's calls, stumbling through her house swinging her bottle of cognac. Throwing pictures of her and Malakai on the floor as she walked to her destination.

She entered the den, with all its glass and crystal, there was a bat signed by Satchel Paige hanging on the wall, she grabbed it and walked over to the door and locked it. She could see herself in the vases, the mirrors anything that could hold her reflection.

Sorrow did not want to see herself, at that moment each item that held her reflection gave her a vision of everything she had done in the past, every enemy flashed before her eyes reminding her of the blood she shed, reminding her that at one point she reigned as the devil in some people's eyes. A feeling of disgust came over her. A feeling of regret for her past actions entered her, starting with her fingers. She could smell the hate and all she wanted to do was destroy the room, she wanted to extirpate the whole world. She waved her hand across the device and through the speakers around her and Mayday ft Tech N9ne's Last One Standing. She let that song and the words enter her body, enter her spirit. A sinister gleam was in her eyes, she had a snare upon her beautiful face.

Sorrow looked at the bat that was swinging in her hand, she raised the bat in a swinging motion, and she took it and swung it at the first vase she saw. Shattering pieces of porcelain with the wooden weapon, pieces flying towards her. Sorrow never worried about the pieces cutting her, her mental was demented at this point, she could not feel anything, she did not hear her husband knocking on the door. Sorrow did not hear when those knocks became demanding and violently harder.

Sorrow swung introducing the bat to the mirror that reflected the visions of Chenille abuse towards her to her and Chenille going at it. The pieces fragmented across the room, a piece flew towards her face slicing her cheek. She still kept going damaging everything breakable in her path. No Rest for the Wicked by Leks Rivers blared through the room as the beating on the door ceased. She did not cease with the destruction of her memories that flickered across the reflective items in that room, this was her house of glass, and she would throw stones or bats in her own glass house.

Sorrow would be damned if she let another mother fucker judge her, punish her for surviving. She would be damned if she let any mother fucker or bitch get away with taken her child, trying to destroy her sanity by endangering the life of her man child.

Anyone who stands in her way of getting her child back and sending the son of bitches to hell that had something to do with it, will be evaporated. If somebody looked suspect, that person will feel her wrath, she would make them feel the same pain or worse than she felt. Innocent blood for innocent blood, eye for an eye, at this point she did not give a flying fuck if this child turned out to be her husband's or her brother's. Either Malakai will handle his business, or she will handle it her way. That boy will be parent less. Sorrow smiled wickedly as she busted out the windows to the french doors leading out to the terrace, overlooking Lake Michigan. She laughed at the memory of her and Malakai making love right on the railing, fucking on the terrace with the sounds of the lake overlapping the carnal cries of euphoria the two of them made.

Sorrow's heart was broken into pieces, such a cliche' term, but it was her truth.

Duke was not Malakai.

Malakai was not Duke.

Damn, my baby boy. A vision of her son popped in her head.

But, in the realm of reality deep down women are attracted to the same type of men, flaws aren't the same, yet similar. Each with weaknesses. Each with strengths.

In a drunken state, a desperate state of mind.

A mind that needed its ego stroked.

A mind that needed to know that she was loved in all her 6 senses.

A mind that needed him to be inside of her, to be reminded that he craved her and only her.

A mind that needed him to show her she deserved to be loved. She deserved to be happy.

Damn, my son! He needs me! I need him!

A mind that needed a moment to escape.

A mind that needed him.

Needed him.

Needs.

Him.

It was just not want.

She needed her husband in carnal way. In a biblical way. In a quench her hydration way. In a fuck her thoughts away way.

Drown her sorrows in feelings, smells and sounds way.

Animalistic. Possessive. Type of way.

Malakai finally made his way through the door. Blood and glass created the path that lead to the cobblestone deck. He can hear the cries of the storm coming from the sky. He can hear the pain of his betrayal screaming out to him from his wife's tears.

He watched her from a distance.

She looked defeated. The rain drowning her white sundress against her skin, making the darkness of her skin seep through the fabric. The translucence of the fabric revealed she was not wearing any under clothes.

The rain reverting her hair back to its natural state, the beauty of her crown still reigned supreme over the rain. He had to make her understand, without saying anything.

He walked out on the deck and lifted her into his arms. He carried her back into the house, stepping over the wrath of sorrow in his journey. Glass, porcelain crackled under his footsteps.

He carried her upstairs to their bedroom, undressed her and then himself.

"Close your eyes, he demanded, How do I like my dick sucked?" he asked.

"Eyes open so you can peer down at me."

"Why?" he whispered as he spooned her

"You like to watch your dick go in and out of my mouth."

"My eyes were closed."

She couldn't get that vision out of her head, so she knew they were closed.

"Where do I like my hands?"

"In my hair."

"Why?"

"You like to run your fingers in my hair while I suck your dick."

"My hands were posted somewhere else."

She remembered, his hands were not touching her.

"How do I like to be when I 'm getting my dick sucked?"

"Naked."

"The only thing that was off was my shirt, even my dick was covered."

She did see a condom on his dick.

"Trust me. You said we were Malcolm X-ing this shit. No matter what we have to do, to get our son back-"

"We will do." She finished his sentence. She knew she couldn't ask him too many questions at this point they didn't know if the kidnappers had cameras or bugs in this house.

She should have killed Alexus.

She would have to kill Alexus.

Malakai trailed kisses down her back,, to her ass and opened her up from the back. He literally was kissing her black ass.

After, their love making Malakai was knocked out with his head on her chest. Sorrow easily moved him to the side and went to the bathroom. She stared at herself in the mirror. She grabbed the scissors and started cutting her shoulder blade length curly hair into a short curly hairstyle. It was now time for her to branch off on her own.

If Alexus had anything to do with Hunter and Se'maj getting kidnapped, what was her motive? Everybody was keeping secrets from her. Truth and her mental state. Nigel and the Underground Playground and her husband with Alexus.

Who else was keeping secrets? Who else would come out the woodwork? When or if Genesis wake up, did she have a secret to tell her? What was Sabrina's secret? All she knew was Sabrina better hope she gets her son back before Sorrow catches up with her.

She kept her cool, thus far, as cool as she could keep it with the rage that was boiling inside of her. Now, it was time for her to take control of the situation.   Black   Pantha   had resurrected.

Chapter 17

She sits down at a table surrounded by a bunch of killers, she smiles at the head killer in charge, dressed in his signature green, she lights the cigar she was offered, takes a puff without coughing and blows it his way, "I'm always on Go!" she told him.

He laughed smugly, "Baby girl, you are playing a game of Checkers when it's Chess. You need to fuck with a real nigga, so I can teach that ass how to play Chess. " He raised his hands as if the laughter of his flunkies was his case and point.

"All this time you niggas thinking Life and this Street shit is a game of Chess. Nah my nigga, when you on a certain level or you are trying to get to a certain level it's a game of Go. Intellectually, Go is more difficult than Chess. Google that shit. "Black Pantha said as she grabbed his bottle of cognac and poured her a drink without asking.

The man beside him took his phone out of his pocket and googled, his face lit up, "She right, yo!" he said trying to show him the phone.

Smack.

The phone flew across the room against the wall.

"Get the fuck out of here. You would be the dumb mother fucker to look that shit up." The Boss curled his lip up at his boy's lame ass action. He pulled out his gun and laid it on the table.

Sorrow pulled out both of her guns, cocked them and laid them on the table. She held his eye contact and lifted one eyebrow, she smirked as to say, "Now what?"

Shaking his head, rubbing his hands together he made a hand movement and his six minions pulled out and aimed at her.

Ready to pull their triggers.

He raised his hand to give the signal.

He wouldn't dare Sorrow thought to herself.

Friends. Enemies. Frenemies.

Who knows these days?

He held it up in the air.

Loyalty.

Who are you loyal too?

Kendrick. Loyalty, Loyalty, Loyalty. The song was now playing in her head. Background music to the spray

of bullets that might be coming her
way.

She did not blink. The look in her
eyes said, I dare you mother fucker!

She grabbed one of his Newports
from off the table, flicking her Bic to
lite it, she inhaled deeply and then
blew out the smoke. His eyes followed
the smoke in the direction she blew it
in, his eyes took in the red dots
plastered on his people's chest, head,
arms. Etc. The six of them looked like
they were coming down with the
chickenpox.

"Touche', mother fucker!" His hand went
down, and they put their weapons up.

"J.Blanco, Sorrow said with a smile and a fist bump.

"What you doing on 5th Block, Queen P?" J. Blanco knew who Sorrow was, she did not have to tell him. He could see it in her eyes when he first met her. He saw it in her eyes when she came to buy those guns. He heard of Black Pantha, and she was the first person he thought of when rumors flew around about this mystery person being a female.

Blanco knew how the King Brothers moved back in the day. He also had an older brother who did moves with C-Note. The way they said Black Pantha orchestrated business is similar to the formula they used. It was a formula that many street hustlers could not execute or did not want to achieve, the art of non-existence.

"I need your assistance."

Blanco excused everyone in the room with a hand wave.

He nodded his head towards her.

"Someone or some people have kidnapped my niece and my son. He wants us to break into the evidence room at County. What he wants, I don't know yet. But, it has something to do with flooding Gary with Haitian imported cocaine. He also says he has a list of

295

dealers he wants me to give the drugs
to. I need your help in all parts of
that. I also need some firepower and
your most trusted, loyal people to be
my man power. In return-"

"Naw, nigga I don't need shit. He
told her cutting her off. They fuck
with yours, they fucking with mine. I'm
down, just guide me through this shit
and tell me what we are dealing with so
far."

Sorrow held up her finger and
answered her ringing phone.

"What up, Shorty!" he said

Sorrow thought she recognized the
voice but not the number, "Frost?"

"Nobody colder, Baby!"

"Frost Bites and Gigabytes!"

"I got you! I also might have a little info for you. I'm going to text you a number for my nigga 2-2 from Dorie Miller. He knows what you need from him! He also has a thing for fucking the right women in the right positions. Give me a quick run down."

"Their holding my son and niece for ransom. Whoever, this is uses an electronic voice. They have been watching us for a long time and now they want us to break into County's evidence room to retrieve some files and items. However, he has not giving me all the information. I think it might be something in what he wants to determine who he is, that is why he is not giving me the information in the files. All I know is he is not working alone, and he is white."

"Nothing wrong with a deadly blizzard in the summer."

"Nothing wrong at all." She ended the call and walked back over to Blanco. Her team was coming together, Malakai won't like it but right now who gives a fuck about his feelings. If he can keep secrets so can she.

"I don't know what I'm up against yet." She confessed

"Now ,neither do they." he said pouring her another drink.

Sorrow was headed back home feeling as if she was finally getting the upper hand on the situation. She finally could smile a little, she was going to get her son back and her niece. She was convinced of it, and she was convinced that her revenge on whoever was behind this was going to be lethal.

Her phone rung, the word Pastor showed up, she didn't answer. She couldn't bring herself to answer the

phone. She realized that they haven't
been to church in the last month.
Sorrow hasn't been in her counseling
sessions within the last month.

God forgive me.

Sorrow pulled over on the shoulder
of the highway, she let out a deep
breath, *Father God, If you would just-*

No, she couldn't promise God that
she wouldn't kill the people behind
stealing her child. She would not fix
her mouth to lie to God, when he
already knew her heart. He already
knows what is going to happen. "Father
God, keep our children safe, cover them

in the blood of Jesus. I- " her phone
started ringing interrupting her
prayer. "Amen" she finished before she
answered her phone.

"It's time to pay the Babysitter.
I want you to put a hundred thousand in
four black garment bags and then place
those bags inside white garbage bags.
The remaining amount put it all in a
black Hefty garbage bag. Place them in
the back of Get'em Girls on the side of
the third dumpster, further away from
the building. I know you got cameras."

"I want to speak to my son and
niece." Sorrow blurted out.

"How about this? You will speak to your NIGGER ass children when I decide you can speak to them. Besides, I'm not finish giving you, your instructions yet."

Sorrow said nothing, she wanted to, but she didn't. She just couldn't wait to kill this white mother fucker. She knew without a doubt this was some racist white mother fucker. There was no telling on how he was treating their children. She had so many concerning questions.

It has been over three weeks since she had seen her child.

Held his hand, kissed his face, heard his laugh. Was he getting fed?

Was he getting bath?

What was going on in his little mind about us not being there with him?

Was he scared, hurt.

Dead.

She wouldn't think like that.

God please stop her from thinking like that.

Snap out of it and focus.

Focus on this mother fucker's demands.

Stay humble, stay humble. Sorrow's stomach turned with deep black generational hate as she held her tongue as he tried to put a noose around her neck with his racist and hateful words that he was weaving into knots to hang her with.

Bitch , be humble! she screamed at herself. The children's lives depended on her to lead with her head and not her feelings.

"Conform to the enemy's tactics until a favorable opportunity offers; then come forth and engage in a battle that shall prove decisive." she quoted the Art of War.

She got her thoughts together and listened without want to say a word.

"You know, it's just like you Niggers to want your reward before you finish the job. Now, listen to me carefully. I want you to take the 10 packages that you have to the evidence room, switch those bricks with the bricks in there. I will text you the number so you can find where it is located in that room. I have names of four dealers and I want you to find them and make them take your product. You are going to find them by hacking into the system. It has entail and pictures of them. The sooner you can get this done, the sooner your little

porch monkeys can come home." He ended
the call.

Looking around the Det. gazed upon
his Beloved and she looked sound
asleep. It was good thing she was
because the alcohol in his system was
making him reckless with his mouth. He
feared what she would do if he found
out that he hated niggers. Not her. He
couldn't hate her. But he still had an
obligation to the white race to take
down as many of them as possible.

Beloved heard everything. She
would play her position until she got
what she wanted. She fed off his hate
for black people. She knew what she was

getting into using him to, she had read his file. She also googled his name and several articles popped up that included him in the mistreatment of black perps, rather they were found to be criminals or not. More than not , he was the Det. on the case that shot , wounded , beat or killed any person of color.

Beloved had questioned him about his new want to have the drugs switched and distributed to known drug dealers around the area. Practically for free, so money was not why he was doing this. She played his explanation back in her head, "I'm setting up the lead Detective on this case."

She felt it was more to it but she didn't give a fuck just as long as her revengeful wrath was done. He wouldn't dare cross her, he worshipped her, no matter how much he hates niggers. A Black woman on his arm and in his bed was his trophy of superiority amongst the Black man. Death comes in many forms of lust, and she was his, he just didn't know it yet.

Chapter 18

"Uuugggggh," her eyes popped open into darkness and buzzing sounds. She woke up feeling violated, violated from the beating and violated from being in the hospital. She had felt every probe, she felt when she was being bathed, she felt when her family was holding her hand and when they were talking to her and about her. But she could not respond, she could not protest.

She was stuck in a white tunnel, but she could hear, feel and smell everything on the outside of her comatose state. What had happened? Well, she knew what happened but, why? She glanced all around to find the board that the nurses write on.

From the date on the board Genesis calculated that she had been in the Hospital a little under a month. It hit her like a Mack truck and tears streamed down her face. Flashes of two people grabbing the kids and running out of her apartment as she was beaten damn near to death. She looked at the time, she had about 5 hours before shift change.

She moved her legs.

Thank God, she could.

She had to find out what happened to her God children.

And she knew just who to start with.

***

Sorrow walked into the Hospital, with a smile on her face, a bouquet of Calla Lilies and balloons in her hand. She was optimistic finally about the situation. She made it to her room, said a prayer and put on a positive attitude for her friend.

Her smile depleted.

The bed was bloody.

The bed was empty.

What the hell happened to her best friend?

To be continued….

Dear Readers, I thank you for your support ,constant pressure and threats to put out another story about Sorrow and Malakai. I know some of you ladies might be disappointed in Malakai, but he is human. To err is human. I appreciate the love you have for my characters. Please email me with your name and proof of purchase of your paperback. Please don't forget your reviews

takeoverpubllc@gmail.com

ms.panthajoneslrb@gmail.com

Mwah Who Loves You Baby!
Ms. Pantha Jones